S·T·E·A·L
A·W·A·Y

Other Apple Paperbacks
you will enjoy:

Afternoon of the Elves
by Janet Taylor Lisle

Cousins
by Virginia Hamilton

The Slave Ship
by Emma Gelders Sterne
and David Lockhart

Risk n' Roses
by Jan Slepian

S·T·E·A·L
A·W·A·Y

Jennifer Armstrong

AN
APPLE
PAPERBACK

SCHOLASTIC INC.
New York Toronto London Auckland Sydney

ISBN 0-590-46921-5

12 11 10 9 8 7 6 5 4 3 2   3 4 5 6 7 8/9

Printed in the U.S.A.   28

First Scholastic printing, September 1993

This book is dedicated,
with love and thanks,
to my parents.

S·T·E·A·L
A·W·A·Y

Manila Hospital
Philippines
July 12, 1928

My dear Free,

   *Will you receive this? I wonder. The mails here are
so unreliable, especially with the rains upon us now.
But even if I were just down the street from you, I
can't be sure you are the same Free, that it is you
I address. Are you? Are you?*

   *There is a new head nurse here at my hospital.
In our first conversation, she mentioned living in
Toronto. To my amazement, she told me of a woman
she knew, by your name, and told me where you were
residing. I looked through the windows and saw not
steamy, rain-washed Manila, but rainy Toronto, and
your face.*

   *It brought back so much to say your name out loud,
and it took me back to the manuscript we labored over
together, and which I have carried with me wherever I
have gone. How hard it was to leave you both! And*

how hard to live from that time without frustration, without many regrets.

Now I have a chance—some chance, perhaps?—of telling you how it was for me back then. I pray that it is you, Free, that your eyes will see these words and you will know at last what I could not say to you then.

With my deepest regard, I remain your friend,

Mary Eleanor Emmons

The account
of the journey of
Susannah McKnight Emmons
and
Bethlehem Reid
as narrated by them.

With notes by Mary Emmons.

1·8·9·6

Until the summer of that year, I had hardly traveled beyond my own neighborhood of Gramercy Park in New York City. In it, I found all the decency and gentility I was raised to expect, and I laughed at the idea of looking further than its graceful precincts.

My dearest friend at that time was Amy Van Tassel. She regularly wrote the most exquisite and inspiring poetry on religious themes, and her mother led a respected temperance committee. From Mrs. Van Tassel I learned to scorn a drunkard for falling from the firm but gentle hand of civilization, and to point him out as an antiexample. I had once, mistakenly, expressed my pity for these wretches, but Mrs. Van Tassel kindly pointed out my error. Now, at the age of thirteen, I knew better.

It was after I had spent an afternoon listening to some highly interesting lectures at the Van Tassels' that my grandmother made her announcement.

"I've had a letter from Bethlehem, and I must go."

Mother and Father shared a look across the supper table.

"I have to go to her," Gran persisted.

"Bethlehem is a place, Gran, not a person," I said. This unexpected sign of age in her troubled me.

She laughed. Mother stood up and began to clear away the supper dishes. It was our Irish girl's night off.

"A place, hmm? That's what you say, Mary," Gran said, shaking her head and smiling at me. "Bethlehem is an old friend in Toronto."

"Toronto? Canada?" I echoed. Gran had often received letters with Toronto as the return address, but I had never thought to ask about her correspondent, nor had she volunteered any information.

"I would very much like you to come with me to see her," Gran added.

"May I?" I turned quickly to my father. He was frowning down at his plate, marshaling a pile of bread crumbs with the flat of his knife. "Father?"

After a pause, he looked up, straight at his mother, my gran. "Is she sick again?"

My grandmother nodded, and the shadow of some deep sadness flickered across her face. "She thinks we should write it all down before she gets much worse," she mused. "I think I agree."

Curiosity was inching me to the edge of my chair, no matter how reserved and temperate I wanted to be. "Gran, who is it? Who's sick?"

"I'll let you decide for yourself who she is," she replied, standing up abruptly. "The train for Toronto leaves at eight in the morning."

I was dumbfounded. Gran was suggesting we leave tomorrow, at the drop of a hat, to pay an unannounced visit to someone I did not know. I wondered what Amy would say.

But I wanted to go.

"Mary is expected for tea at the Reverend Brown's tomorrow," Mother said from the doorway. "He is from one of the finest families in New York City—"

"And Bethlehem Reid is one of the finest women in the world," my grandmother said, her back straight and stubborn. "I have invited Mary to visit her."

Mother's face colored. "An old slave? Mother Emmons, I hardly think—" She broke off as Father shook his head. With a frown, she turned and fussed with the gas lamp.

"A slave?" I whispered.

My grandmother took my shoulder in a sudden grip. "She's not a slave, Mary! She is not!"

Her fierceness deepened my confusion. I wasn't to understand what my grandmother was talking about for some time. It took the long train ride to Toronto, meeting Bethlehem Reid, and helping Gran and Bethlehem write their story down, before I knew what she meant. Not just that Bethlehem was no longer in bondage, but that she truly never had been.

And my grandmother, Susannah McKnight Emmons, had good reason to know that, too. When she began her history on the train, however, I was far from recognizing the truth.

WINTER
1·8·5·5

SUSANNAH: I think you know, Mary, that I was born on a small farm near Bennington, Vermont. I lived there as puppies and colts do, without knowing that there was any way of living except joyfully, any way of being except loved and protected, until my parents were killed. The thaw was treacherous that February, coming suddenly as it did. The ice on our pond gave way beneath them as they held hands and pointed to the hills. I saw this from the window of my bedroom, where I was confined with a grippe. They were gone before I reached the stairs.

I remember that it didn't seem to me the fire in the sugar house could still be smoking or the hens in the barn still complaining about the cold, without my parents there to see it and make it go on, day by day. My grippe rapidly worsened to pneumonia from clutching at the broken ice in only my night shift, and I was in a fever for many days. When I awoke on the seventh day, my parents were in the ground and my uncle was waiting to take me to Virginia.

The fever and the suddenness of my parents' deaths had left me weak and uncertain. I walked and sat and ate and lay down, not knowing if the earth would be changed when I woke up, if the clouds would be on fire or water turn to grasshoppers in my cup. It seemed to me that if my parents could be gone so suddenly, anything might happen.

So three days of traveling might as well have been three weeks: I did not know where I was. Towns, and the names of towns, flowed past the train windows. The meager coal stove in our car leaked eye-stinging fumes. Near to it the air was hot and breathless, and ten feet away the cold squeezed me into my corner. Passengers were forever coughing and wiping their eyes. One man swore he would break a window, but the others, irritable from the cold, shouted him down.

My uncle, whom I quickly learned was a minister as relentless and stern and sparing of words as his God, had precious little to say to me. I dogged him through the cavernous iron depots in New York and Baltimore, made the change at Manassas Junction, and ached on an endless series of hard wooden seats. I was utterly wretched.

The noise of the train is with me even now. It never stopped, you see, as even in the depots gasps of steam, the frequent ringing of iron on iron, and arcane rail-road terms shouted between trainmen, filled the air. In motion, the train alternately galloped across level fields, ground up hills, or stumbled through junctions. The sounds filled my head, and between that and the hiss of my fever, I had to close my eyes and pray for sleep. I was a prey to every grief in the calendar.

It was only as we neared Front Royal that I felt the fist of a new worry press in on my stomach. Vermont was a free state. Virginia was not. Reverend Mason, back home, had said slavery was an abomination in the eyes of God. Every Sunday of my life the words *slavery* and *sin* were uttered in the same breath. To what was I going now?

"Uncle," I asked, squeezing my knees together. "How many—"

He closed his Bible on one finger. "How many what?"

Across the aisle, a fat man with a greasy coat collar took out a pocket watch and scowled at it.

"Slaves?" I whispered.

"Ten. Only those in the house will concern you. You'll have no traffic with the hands outside."

The train lurched around a bend, throwing me against the wooden armrest. I held on tight as the car swung back the other way. I feared for my soul; therefore, I realized that I *could* not be a slaveholder. And yet my uncle himself was a man of God. Was it possible, I wondered, to be godly and righteous while owning slaves, while committing this dreadful sin? I could not credit it. I could not reconcile this contradiction. I could only commend myself to God's care. I prayed He was watching over me.

"You may wish to see to your feminine needs before we leave the station in Front Royal," he went on. He was looking over the top of my head.

My feminine needs were a source of the profoundest mystery to me at that time, at thirteen—just your age now, Mary. But I nodded my comprehension. I was anxious for a privy, I can tell you that.

I was waiting for more from him, but my uncle was clearly finished with me. He was a man to instruct, not converse. Blinking hard, I looked out the window again and bumped my head on the sooty glass as the train swung heavily into another curve. My stockings itched horribly from fleas and the days of travel. My own odor and the reek of soggy wool assaulted me with every breath. I scratched my head once and came away with a rim of coal dust under the nail. You only know these modern trains, with their carpeting and gaslights and porters to look after us. But believe me, in 1855, to travel by train was to test the limits of endurance against the necessities of time.

But when we arrived in Front Royal, at dusk, I balked at leaving that train. Before me was a confusion of noises, smells, animal complaints, and people. On every side, bodies jostled through the crowd, yelling for the stationmaster, yanking children, arguing over crates.

And everywhere I looked were slaves. I had seen

Negroes before, of course. There were freedmen—a few—in Bennington. But to me, the condition of these Front Royal slaves loomed as large in my imagination as though they stood wrapped in chains. In fact, they merely carried sacks, or stood at the heads of nervous horses, or stepped out of white folks' way. I was terrified of them.

"Susannah!"

Behind me, my uncle barked my name like a warning, and I nearly fell out onto the platform. For a moment, I thought I might cry. The man who was now my guardian picked up my box and strode through the crowd. A wall of woolen coats instantly closed around him, and I was left to fight my way through. A riding crop poked me in the eye, and a gesturing man stepped backward onto my foot. My eye smarted, my toes throbbed, and I knew a moment of panic. Then I gathered my skirts and plunged into the crowd after my uncle.

When I found him, he was waiting in a wagon. An old black man was putting my articles in it, and my uncle was making a study of a news sheet. He saw me, and waved with it onto the seat. I scrambled up with unwomanly haste and made myself as small as I could. The wagon tipped wildly as the driver pulled himself up.

"Make time, Monday," my uncle told him. "It's already late."

The slave called Monday touched his whip to the

horse's withers, and we jolted off. I wanted to speak to him, but I dared not, nor did I know what I would say if I dared. I stared at the back of his neck, which was seamed and stitched with many lines above his coarse cotton shirt. I knew he must be cold, and without knowing why, I took off my mittens. I knew I could not give them to him, but I had some confused thought that I should go without them myself. My fingers were soon numb, but I somehow fell asleep.

"Is this her? Father, is this Susannah?"

Those were the first words I heard my cousin Fidelia speak. Even in befuddled waking, I thought there was a sharpness to her voice. I struggled to open my eyes and see her. She was one year older than I was; I knew only that.

"Are you awake, child?" came an older voice, my aunt Reid. "Susannah McKnight! Can you hear me?"

I blinked as a lamp bobbed near and then floated away. I could make out people, but no faces. It was very dark, and a damp breeze chilled my neck.

"How do you do?" I said, although to my own ears my voice sounded muffled through layers of cloth.

The lamp bobbed near again, and I could see a round, surprised face, and dark ringlets beneath lace. "Gracious," Aunt Reid said. "You're awake!"

"I'm sorry," I mumbled. I tried to stand but found my legs would not comply. Hands reached out to me and lifted me down. Overhead, bare branches rattled.

"Child! How distressing your grief and this journey must have been!" Aunt Reid exclaimed. "But your travail has ended. God has delivered you safely into our care."

"More like it was father," came a young man's warm and teasing voice from far away.

"Oh, Byron." Aunt Reid sighed.

As I stood uncertainly among the shadows by the wagon, I peered into the dark where my elder cousin stood. The lamplight touched on several people but left the faces obscured. I prayed I was dreaming: the night sounds and odors, even the dusty feel of the ground, were strange to me. I needed something familiar and real, as a drowning man needs air. A tall figure strode toward us.

"Pa!" I gasped, stumbling.

A startled silence closed in around the company. I turned my head away when I saw the man was my uncle. My stomach twisted.

"Poor child," Aunt Reid murmured. Her soft arms encircled my shoulders. "She's near swooning with exhaustion."

I tried to say, "No, I'm not," but my tongue would not serve me. I thought perhaps she was right. My fever had not entirely loosed its grip.

Ahead of us, a lighted doorway stood out of the darkness. My feet touched dirt, then stone, then wood, and I was in the hallway. Five slaves stood waiting, lamplight throwing half of each face into shadow. I could not look at them, but focused on the patterned carpet, the squares of red and green.

"We have an especial surprise," Fidelia cried out. She rustled suddenly into the light, and I saw her as a younger image of her mother: round face, dark ringlets, lace. Her sharp eyes fixed on mine.

"Can I show you now?" she asked. "Can I show her, Mother? Now, directly?"

I did not trust myself to speak, but I followed her with my eyes. She flounced behind a door and popped out again, dragging someone with her.

"She used to be mine, but I'm letting you have her for your own," Fidelia crowed. She shoved a slim black girl toward me. "Beth, here's your new miss."

Bethlehem and I locked eyes for the first time, and I burst into tears.

1·8·9·6

My grandmother stopped speaking, and I looked up. A steady downpour outside the train made the interior dim and shadowed.

"I'm not tired," I said, raising my pencil. "I can keep writing."

Gran was staring out the rain-streaked window of our train. We had recently passed through Buffalo, where once great piles of hides had been unloaded on the platforms. Gran pinched the bridge of her nose, her eyes closed.

"I'm tired, Mary. No more for now." She gave me a brief smile. "We'll wait until we reach Toronto. When we see Bethlehem, we can continue."

I was anxious to hear more of the story that minute. I marveled that until then I had known nothing of it, that she had kept it hidden inside her. Gran had always been just Gran to me, the facts and fulfillments of her life plain enough for anyone to read. I was hurt that she had not considered me old enough or wise enough to tell. I felt she should know this, but I would not tell her.

Resisting a sigh, I gazed out the window, too. I was thinking of her, an orphaned girl, taking another train into a frightening future forty years earlier. I thought I knew something of what her future was to be—wife of an honest farmer and mother of three—but that young Susannah had known nothing of what was to come. She had been traveling to Bethlehem, and now I was, too.

We took a hack from the depot, and I was disappointed that Toronto looked more or less like New York, like our own neighborhood in Gramercy Park. We passed dry goods stores, butchers, a news office, all gray and monotonous in the rain. The address Gran had given the driver was in a block of shabby rooming houses, each with several names on the door.

"Reid, Miss B. This is it," Gran said.

I knew it had been the custom for slaves to be given the family name of the slaveowner. It had always struck me as a perverted sort of adoption, and it did so again as I looked at Bethlehem's name on the door.

Gran's cheeks were flushed, and she pressed her hands against them.

"Gran? Are you feeling well?" I asked her.

She nodded wordlessly. The landlady answered our knock and directed us up three flights of stairs. I stopped with Gran on each landing while she caught her breath; her eyes strained upward into the dimness. There was a damp chill in the air.

"I'll go on, if you like," I told her. She looked so old to me. "I can ask them for a glass of water."

She nodded again, and smiled. "Tell her I'm coming as fast as my heart will let me."

My heart tripped inside me. I did not want my grandmother in this place with stained wallpaper and cabbage smells. My mother would never have walked in.

I left Gran and hurried up the last flight. I found *Reid, Miss B.* again on a door and knocked hard.

When it opened, a black girl, seeming about my age, stood before me. She regarded me cautiously, her dark eyes tilted up at the corners, her mouth tilted down.

"Bethlehem?" I whispered.

"Miss Bethlehem is in bed," she told me. Her hand twisted the doorknob slowly first one way, then the next. "What do you want with her?"

I blushed at making such a foolish mistake. Of course Bethlehem was a woman Gran's age.

Gran appeared at the top of the stairs then, and came breathlessly toward us. With relief, I turned away from the girl's suspicious eyes and let my grandmother assume charge.

"I'm an old friend of Miss Reid's," Gran said. She met the girl's look steadily, smiling and catching her breath. "She's expecting me, I believe. I'm Mrs. Emmons."

"Ah—" A short sound escaped the girl. She closed her mouth quickly, but she nodded.

"Do you help Miss Reid?" Gran asked. She did honestly want to know, I could see that.

"I'm Free."

It took me a moment to see she meant her name, odd as it was. Gran smiled, her glance darting to a closed door beyond. "Is she awake, Free?"

Free stepped back and gestured with one hand into the apartment, while Gran murmured her thanks and moved past her. I was hurrying after when Free stopped me in the middle of the room with one hand on my arm. I looked at her in surprise.

"Wait," she said, taking away her hand.

"But—" I watched my grandmother tap once on the closed door and then slip inside.

Two voices pitched low reached our ears. Free was standing, head bent, listening. I looked around me. The room was small, or seemed so, with books piled everywhere and overflowing the shelves. A small, ugly oil lamp occupied the center of the round table, and three unmatched chairs crowded around. Yellow curtains of cheap muslin hung at the single window, but I could see a mean, poor view beyond, muddy looking and wet. In one corner, half-hidden by a screen, was a narrow, neatly made bed. My sense of good manners kept me from asking if Free actually lived and slept there.

It was the books, therefore, that I decided to examine. There was a startling wealth of them, and I picked up the nearest one to me, *Moby Dick*.

"Does Miss Reid read all these books?" I asked for something to say. I felt Free watching. I thought she might take the book from me.

"Yes," she answered hotly. "She teaches us all how to read. That's what she is, a teacher."

"Oh." I pretended to read the first page of *Moby Dick*, but my ears were straining for the sound of Gran's step. I very much wanted her to call for me.

Free made an awkward movement with her hands. "You could sit."

"Oh, thank you," I breathed, remembering to smile. Free glanced away. I sat and then turned pages at regular intervals.

"Mary!" Gran stood in the doorway. Her eyes looked red to me, but she was smiling. A tendril of her white hair had come loose and curled over her shoulder. "Come, meet Bethlehem."

Free stood up and took two steps. "She gets tired, ma'am."

"I know. Thank you. Come here, Mary."

I did not look at Free as I passed her. Gran slipped one arm across my shoulders and led me into the bedroom.

What was I expecting? I knew little of Bethlehem so far but that my grandmother would answer a summons to travel from New York City to Toronto to see her. A tall, regal woman, proud of carriage and showing her dignity and quality in every gesture? Or some faded embodiment of slavery days, a granny in a head scarf?

"Hello," she said, rising from the bed. She came toward me, and I stopped. We regarded each other in silence.

She was tall, but not very. Her hair was pulled severely back, and the collar of her white blouse threw her skin into dark contrast. A small silver brooch of poor quality was pinned at her throat. Her eyes rested on mine thoughtfully. Without warning, she reached one hand to my cheek and held it there. Her skin was cool and dry. She traced my cheekbone with one finger. No one spoke.

I glanced anxiously at Gran. I did not know what to say. No black person had ever touched me so before, and although I was not alarmed, I was considerably surprised.

"She looks like you," Bethlehem said in a voice warm with wonder. She smiled suddenly, and I couldn't help smiling back.

Gran came forward, her skirts swishing gently. "I think she's like me—I hope so, at least," she added with a smile for me.

Puzzled, but also happy, I looked from my grandmother to the elderly woman before me. I could only wait for explanations.

"Is she ready to hear this story?" Bethlehem asked, frowning at me. I was sure she didn't see me, not really. Her eyes were faraway, in another time.

"We've already started," Gran said. "Why don't you read what I've told her so far, and you add to it where I've gone wrong."

Bethlehem cast Gran a swift, amused glance. "You always did like tales."

They both laughed, and Bethlehem coughed into a handkerchief. I was still perplexed, but glad to be useful. I took our papers out of the valise I still held.

"Here it is," I offered.

Bethlehem ran her eyes down it quickly. "You write a fine hand, Miss Mary," the teacher in her said. "High marks."

I laughed, although I did not know why. Briefly, I wondered what Amy Van Tassel would think of my being praised by this woman. And then I realized I didn't care in the least.

"We should sit in the other room," Bethlehem said, looking from me to the pages of dictation. "Free needs to hear this, too."

WINTER
1·8·5·5

BETHLEHEM: "Here's your new miss," Miz Fidelia told me. I felt a power of discouragement settle on me when I saw my new miss then. Susannah was bawling, red in the face, her yellow braids straggling apart. A sorry sight. I had heard of Yankees being angels of deliverance who could spirit slaves away to a free place called Canada. But here was one no bigger than me, and probably not as strong. There would be no deliverance through this Yankee.

"Where's your manners, Beth? Look sharp!" Miz Fidelia used the chance to pinch my arm. Any excuse was enough for that girl. Mean as a wasp, she was, and I was glad to be handed over.

How old was I then? My blood had not come yet, but did so not much after, so I expect I was the age of you girls now. I had lived at Reids' Farm for some years, and had a rememory of some other place like a place in a dream. There were women there I called Mama. But I had come to Reids' alone, without kin. It seemed I had always been waving flies off Miz Fidelia, making clothes for Miz Fidelia, fetching water for Miz Fidelia, being slapped by Miz Fidelia. I had learned to tolerate her the way I tolerate the heat: nothing to do but wait for it to pass.

"Why's she crying so, Mother?" Miz Fidelia whined. The girl knew how to pout. "Don't she care for Beth?"

Miz Reid gathered up Susannah with a cluck. "It may be she has a brain fever from traveling. I shall put her to bed myself. You may go, Beth."

I could not stop myself from looking at Miz Reid, Miz Reid who could not pick up her own needle from the floor without calling on a body to do it for her.

Miz Fidelia saw me and slitted her eyes. "None of your sass," she hissed.

Lizer, Monday, Betty's Tim, and the others had melted away, quiet as owls. Mass Reid's boots stepped hard and slow across the parlor floor. I waited.

"Come now," Miz Reid crooned. Susannah hiccuped and rubbed her nose. I do not think she saw any of us at all.

I watched them go, and then I walked out of the ring of lamplight. I knew my way down the dark hall and on out to the back door. Outside the air was still sharp. I walked on to my garden patch and stood where it was sheltered and white with the moon.

"My cousin looked poorly," Mass Byron said out of the darkness nearby.

I nearly jumped a foot, but then went quiet and still. "A body gets tired" was all I said.

"That's true." His shape came nearer. He was very near me. He was silent.

"I got to go," I told him, stepping aside.

"Beth! Stay. Ain't I always kind to you?"

I swallowed hard. There was nothing I could say to that. Kind? He told me I was honey; then he gave me his boots to black. Mass Byron was there whenever I raised my eyes, and his attentions were starting to fetch me pinches from Miz Fidelia even more than was regular.

She had taken up tagging after her brother. He had taken up tagging after me. It got so I couldn't sweep the porch or hunt eggs without stepping around Mass Byron. Then Miz Fidelia would turn the corner like a bitch dog sniffing for her hound, and he would ease off. She hated the sight of me, which was how she could make her cousin Susannah here such a kind-hearted gift. I thought I was shut of her, and thanked the Lord.

I wasn't shut of Byron, though. And I didn't see how I could be. I was young, but not too young to know he could take what he wanted if he was of a mind to. If he said sit, I'd be bound to sit. And if he said lie yourself down, I'd be bound to do that, too. It made me tremble, and my face burned with shame and confusion. I had some hope that Byron could love me and give me my freedom. But even then I had a sense that freedom was something I had to take for myself, to make it stick.

"Beth," he said again. He kicked a pumpkin shell, and the old vines hissed and twisted around our feet. "I never would treat you hard."

I still did not answer. I turned my face away and turned my mind to God. Didn't my Lord deliver Daniel? I was in a lion's den—I knew that.

By and by, Mass Byron wearied of what wasn't happening. He went off, sulky as a mule.

And I—I just had to pray. I sank to my knees, and the smell of the cool wet earth rose up to my face. There were bones in the ground, bones of jays and raccoons, Indians and white people, bones and fur and blood. That is what I smelled in the earth, in the earth that I brought to my cheek. And what I prayed was this: let my bones be here, too. Let it be soon, Lord. I don't want to do this life no more.

SUSANNAH: That first night my aunt put me to bed. She fussed at me and poor-orphaned me so that sleep left entirely. When she finally took the lamp and went out, I was wide awake and staring in a small room to the rear of the house.

Mother. Father. I can't tell you how I missed them. The ache of self-pity and grief I was feeling must come forth, I thought, in a wild howl to the stars. Fear and lonesomeness loomed over me like shades from Hell. With a groan, I fought my way free of the bedclothes and stumbled to the window.

Beyond, moonlight froze the landscape: everything was a ghost of itself. Tears wet my cheeks. I was speaking, but did not know my own words. Then, by degrees, I made out a figure below me, by the rude cabins out back. It seemed to me in my despair that this person was myself. She stood utterly alone, her face raised to heaven and her arms straight by her sides.

As I watched, she sank to her knees with bowed head. Her hands moved along the ground in front of her. Lifted, her hands let slip what they grasped, then reached down and grasped it again. I could feel that rich soil, smell its loamy breath, as she raised her hands to her face and rested her cheek on the earth in her palm.

A sudden stillness came upon me. I knew at last that I could pray. But then it seemed to me that I had prayed already and taken comfort from it. She stepped out of the moonlight into shadow again, and I went to my bed to sleep.

I did not know at the time that it was Bethlehem I saw, only that the figure was as desolate as I. But when I awoke before dawn, I felt I was not utterly alone. I dragged a chair to the window and crouched there, waiting for the first glimpse of this place that would be my home, wondering what this new day would bring. After a moment of strain, I shoved the window open a few inches and breathed deeply. The air was still quite cold.

A thin line of light crept along the eastern horizon. Fitful birdsong broke out among the pines and oaks. Soon I could make out ranks of fence posts fading into the mist, and broad sweeps of brown pasture. The principal crops on my uncle's farm were hams and horses. Somewhere out there were sows and boars still snoring and kicking in heavy sleep. Corn stubble stretched for acres. Barns, corncribs, sheds, smokehouses—and what I soon saw were slave cabins—huddled together in the rising light. A horse neighed.

Then, as I watched, a woman came to the door of one cabin. She stretched, ignoring the chickens that cluttered around at her appearance. Someone still within the cabin must have spoken to her, because I saw her turn, listening, and let out a laugh. She shook her head and went in again.

The old man, Monday, rounded a corner, walking stiffly and rapping at doorposts as he came. Two hounds loped after him. I observed these stirrings with some perplexity. The slaves' activity was entirely unremarkable. They woke up, dressed, started work. The horrors of which I had heard were nowhere in sight.

But when Bethlehem stepped from the last cabin, I ducked below the sill. My pulse sped while I peeked out to see *my* slave. I shuddered; the gorge rose in my throat at the words; the sight of her filled me with dread.

"Dear Lord." I clasped my hands. "Tell me how to suffer this. Please know I didn't ask them to give her to me. I don't want her. I can take care of myself—I truly can. I don't want her."

I peeked out again, but Bethlehem was gone. The notion that she might be coming to my room threw me into a flurry. I snatched up my discarded traveling clothes and searched for a place to hide them. Breathless, I tossed them into the wardrobe. I flung the counterpane over the rumpled bed, then changed my mind and jumped in again. I closed my eyes, feigning sleep.

You can laugh at me now, but I lay there for some long minutes, curled in a ball and listening to the blood pound in my ears. As the time passed and no one appeared, I began to feel foolish and relieved, both. I opened my eyes.

The morning had well and truly arrived. A wan light filled my room. I began to wonder what was expected of me. Should I stay abed until called for? Dress and venture forth? Undecided, I pulled on my shoes. Then I stood by the open window in my night shift and shoes, with a shawl about my shoulders, and gazed, shivering, out at my new home.

A distant shout drew my attention to a paddock. Three horses burst through the mist, kicking and tossing manes. A mare, heavy with foal, ambled more slowly after them with sedate nods of her head. The farm was revealed to me as a broad spread of cultivated land surrounded by dense forest. The blue hills rose on every side. It was lovely, I tell you, profoundly beautiful. I knew it was good land, and yet my parents' farm, for all its rocks and stubborn stumps, was the better place. My parents would have broken the land with their empty hands rather than yoke a single slave.

I turned away and pulled my stained clothes out of the wardrobe. They were all I had. My boxes had not been brought up.

The door opened behind me. Bethlehem stood there, looking at the dress I held.

"I can brush that for you," she said in a low voice.

My throat was tight. I shook my head. "You don't have to do for me," I told her.

"I do, miss."

"No, but—" I backed up, holding the dress against me.

Bethlehem just stood there. "I'll brush it for you." Her face moved not a whit in expression. She did not look at my eyes.

I was backed into the wall and still shaking my head. With a gulp, I said, "Beth—your name is Beth, isn't it?"

"It's what they call me, miss."

"I know a girl named Betsy," I babbled. I know I

gave her a pathetical smile. "Least, I knew her. At home. I come from Vermont, way up North."

"Yes, miss," Bethlehem said.

She knelt by the bed and reached under. She withdrew the chamber pot with the chipped porcelain lid, and I felt my face flare up.

"I'm sorry," I whispered.

She stared at me for a moment. It was her turn to shake her head. "Your boxes is still downstairs. I can bring them up for you."

Before I could speak, she left the room. Tears scalded my cheeks. I crushed my dress against my face. Did God see me and know I didn't choose this? How could I ever bear it? I knew I could not stay.

1·8·9·6

I was still writing down Gran's words, although my
hand was painfully cramped by now. Gran saw me
flex it, and she paused in her narration.

"Mary, forgive me," she said.

"Maybe just a little rest?" I asked, looking from her
to the others.

Bethlehem rose. "Free can spell you, Mary, and the
two of you can take it in turns. Free, if you would
please fetch some water, we can make tea. I've saved
some."

Free left her chair in an instant and took the kettle
from a small burner at the back of the room. I do not
know how far she had to go for the water, down how
many flights of stairs. But she flew to answer Bethlehem's request. She had not spoken once so far, but
her face had been expressive of many things. I sat
where I was, gazing absently out at the rain. My
hands were cold as well as tired.

Gran was slowly shaking her head. Her eyes were

still filled with memories. "That first morning was a Sunday. I should have known from my uncle's impatience. I didn't know what day it was that I had arrived, but after I dressed I soon knew why he was so rushed. He had a sermon to preach."

Her bitter tone told me what she thought of her uncle's ministry. I had never known her to be disrespectful of the clergy, and I hardly knew what to say.

"Some number of years ago, I discovered an 1860 edition of some of his sermons in a small shop," Gran said, reaching into her reticule. "He was very highly regarded, and his sermons were published in many parts of the South."

She handed the small volume across the table to me. A slip of paper marked a page.

"Read that one," Gran suggested. "It is representative. It might as well be any one that I heard during my time in Front Royal."

I raised my eyes to Bethlehem, who was moving quietly about the room, finding tea in a canister, taking a sugar bowl from a shelf, lighting a match from a small hoard. With mingled curiosity and trepidation, as though overturning a stone in some dank and fetid place, I read to myself the first words on the page.

I take as my text today the words of Leviticus: "Both thy bond-men and thy bond-maidens which thou shalt have shall be of the heathen that are around you; of them ye shall buy bond-men and bond-maids; and ye shall

take them as an inheritance for your children after you;
they shall be your bond-men forever."

Blushing hotly, I looked up at Gran. She shook her
head. "Aloud, please."

"No, Gran!" I turned my gaze mutely to Bethlehem's back.

"They are not your words, Mary," Gran said.

Free returned then, with the kettle of water. She
placed it on the gas burner, and stood by it, waiting.
The silence grew.

"Gran." My voice shamed me. I would not look at
Free.

"Go on, Mary," Gran pressed, frowning and smiling at the same time. "Read it. Don't fret yourself."

To please her, I would read it. But my tongue was
as heavy as a stone.

" 'Our brethren to the North,' " I read, " 'have the
temerity to question the plan of Almighty God. Has
not God decreed in his wisdom that slavery is both
right and fit? By his laws and ordinances, he has set
his hand upon the shoulder of the master and said
unto him, "They shall be your bond-men forever."

" 'Our northern critics say God instructed us to take
the *heathen* into bondage; yet is not the black man
among us brought into the community of God? Such
is the charge of the man from Massachusetts and the
man from New York.

" 'But I say to him that the black man and the tribes

of Africa, tho' they may profess to love God as true and righteous Christians, are the very descendants of Canaan, sons of Ham, the accursed son of Noah. And God said, "Cursed be Canaan; a servant of servants shall he be unto his brethren." It is ordained by God himself that the black man shall be held in perpetual bondage to the white man.' "

My thoughts spiraled wildly.

I heard Bethlehem draw a breath and let it out bit by bit.

"It goes on in a similar vein," I whispered, miserably.

Free put cups and saucers on the table with such force that the dishes clattered and jumped. My back prickled in the stillness that followed.

"I don't have so many dishes that you can smash them all up, remember," Bethlehem said to Free. Then, turning to me she added, "Go on, Mary. Let's just listen to the rest."

Gran was sitting with bowed head. While Free grudgingly took her place at the table, I cleared my throat to continue.

" 'Our Lord Jesus came to fulfill the laws of God, not to overturn them! Thus, as slavery is held in God's favor and esteem, they sin mightily who seek to abolish our sanctified institution.

" 'Therefore, my friends, fear God and obey him. Treat your servant as you should. Turn your face from those who tread the paths of damnation. Cleave unto our laws in all righteousness.

" 'In the name of our Lord, Jesus Christ. Amen.' "

My voice was a thread, and my throat ached horribly. My heart burned that the Bible could be perverted so. Those words were Scripture, and yet I knew they must be wrong. Everyone knew slavery was wrong.

I raised my head proudly, only to find Free staring at me, as at a snake or a dead thing.

"It's not true," I said, looking straight back at Free and speaking with conviction. "It's just not true. God didn't mean it that way at all."

She took in a sharp breath. "I don't need you to tell me that," she said. Her voice was bitter, and her eyes filled with anger toward me.

"Free," Bethlehem warned. She stood up to pour the tea water, and Free stood with her. The words had stung me like barbs, and still smarted. Who was Free to accuse me? I didn't even know what she was doing here.

I looked beseechingly at Gran. Why had she subjected me to such an ordeal? I thought I would weep with the hurt and humiliation of it.

She shook her head. "The slaves heard that, too," she pointed out. "Think how it must have broken their hearts to be told it was God's plan they should suffer."

"But *I'm* not a slave or a master," I said fiercely. "Why did you make me read it?" My chin began to shake, and I could not stop the tears from sounding in my voice.

"Mary."

I would not look at my grandmother. I could not forgive her for it and turned away. She had not done unto me as she would have others do unto her, but I would not quote scriptures at her. My neck ached. Free went to the gray window and stared out.

"Seems like all he talked about was the black *man* and the white *man*," Bethlehem said in a mild voice as she set a crockery teapot on the table. "I guess he plain forgot there were black women and white women in the world."

She and Gran laughed and shook their heads at their memories, but I was adamant and did not care to be lightened. Free had not rejoined us. Her back was taut and implacable.

"Free, why don't you take a turn writing," Bethlehem suggested. She rose and joined Free by the window and placed one hand gently on Free's shoulder. "Please."

Raindrops tapped forlornly against the panes. I cupped my hands around my tea for warmth.

Free looked up at last. Her expression softened. "Are you sure you aren't getting too tired?" she asked Bethlehem in a quiet voice. "You don't want to rest for a while?"

"No, child," Bethlehem said with a smile. "I'm tougher than you think."

I was puzzled by their exchange. Was Free there to look after Bethlehem, or was it the other way round? As Free returned to the table, I passed along the paper and pen and stole a look at her. I wondered who she was.

WINTER
1·8·5·5

BETHLEHEM: That Sunday after Susannah arrived, there was a camp meeting in a field outside of town. There were many of those revivals, and Miz Reid never missed one, no matter what the weather. But I remember that one because of Susannah's arrival. Miz Reid took Miz Fidelia and Susannah off with her directly after church. I knew what to expect when they returned.

I was in the winter kitchen with Lizer, mixing bread pudding for supper. I heard rain begin talking to the kitchen roof as Miz Reid came in, looking like she had gone through the briars backward. Her hair had a clawed-at aspect. Her face was red with tears.

"Come into the parlor," she gasped. Her voice was hoarse with the heaving of her bosom. "We must pray."

Lizer began to shake her head. "No, ma'am. I got to get the supper ready."

"Beth!"

Before I could think of what to say, she had my hand and was dragging me along with her. Miz Fidelia and Susannah were in the parlor; Miz Fidelia began a sorry lament as soon as her mother appeared. Susannah stood in the corner like a kicked dog, struck dumb and cowering.

"Lord, save us," Miz Reid moaned, falling to her knees at my feet. "We shall surely spend eternity damned for our sins. I know I shall die soon! God's judgment shall be upon all our house! Pray with us, Beth! Pray!"

Her crying was wild and crazy, and her nails tore into my ankles again and again. I did not know what to say. I agreed with her: I was sure my God would send her and all her kind to Hell for their wickednesses, just as sure as the slaves would find freedom with the angels on the right hand of the Lord. I wanted to say, "Yes, King Jesus!" and raise my arms. But the creature at my feet turned my stomach. It sickens me even now.

"He hath scattered the proud in the imagination of their hearts," she moaned. "He hath put down the mighty from their seats and exalted them of low degree!"

The two girls gaped at me, and at Miz Reid. Susannah was as scared and pale as a homeless ghost, and Miz Fidelia nearly killed me with her eyes. Her mother pulled me down with all the strength of her fear of Hell. I kneeled with her, and prayed for them all to die. Yes, I did.

In answer to my prayer, the rain began to beat at the windows in sudden bursts like the lashes of a whip. Miz Reid groaned and clutched at her heart. She fell into a fit.

"Look what you did," Miz Fidelia cried. She pushed me aside and helped her mother to rise. "Mother, you should be in your bed."

"I'm not well," Miz Reid said, fluttering her eyes. "Fidelia? Are you there?"

The girl sent me a spiteful look. "I'm here, Mother," she said in a honey voice. "Let me help you. God will spare you to us yet, Mother. You are so good."

Weeping together, mother and daughter left the room. In the silence, I heard my blood race through me blindly, a wild animal trying to dash out of a trap. I still crouched on the floor where Miz Reid had dragged me down.

"You're bleeding," Susannah whispered, wide-eyed. I saw her throat jump, and she pointed to my ankles. "She cut you."

Long lines of blood crossed my ankles where my mistress's scratching had broken the skin. In that lamplight, the shining drops looked as dark as I was.

"Are my bones black, too?" I asked, staring down.

"I don't think so," Susannah said somberly, as though I had asked her. "I think all bones are white."

I stared at her and felt something inside me—a laugh, a scream, I did not know.

"No, they ain't," I told her. Then I left.

SUSANNAH: That camp meeting terrified me. My aunt had succumbed to a frenzy of morbid weeping, and my cousin had huddled with some other girls and stared at me, speaking behind her hands. I made no attempt to join them. Under the tent, the traveling preacher exhorted the crowd to repentance, and many of them were prostrated with fear and the evil in their own hearts. If I had been in a cage with wild savages, I could not have been more dismayed. Small wonder that Bethlehem was so disgusted by my aunt, by my cousin, by me. I know we do seem a pitiful lot, in the telling.

In any event, my aunt cultivated the weakness of body and spirit that the meeting had brought on: she remained closeted in her room for days with the drapes pulled shut. My cousin Fidelia also indulged in a debilitating condition of her own. She was therefore able to neglect her needlework and recline in the parlor most of the day, from time to time calling out in wilting tones for Byron to read to her from the Bible or the latest *Godey's Lady's Book. Godey's* was just as popular a magazine then as it is now, and Fidelia hoarded each issue.

And, as my uncle had frequent business in town and was seldom seen before evening, it was Byron who introduced me to the place. He found me pacing forlornly on the porch that second day and, with many apologies, took me in charge.

"You look like a dory adrift in the lake," Byron said. "Nobody's looking after you?"

I had a piece of twig in my hands that I was steadily chipping into bits. The last pieces fell to the porch floor as I shook my head.

Byron smiled. I could not help smiling back. My cousin was seventeen, and handsome, and he had very winning ways. I began to imagine he might make my exile less harsh. He raised a brass spyglass to his eye and examined me. My face warmed under his scrutiny. What a charmer he was.

"Come along with me," he said, offering his arm with another smile. "I'll show you how we contrive to live around here."

Shyness held my tongue still. Byron looked down at me and arched one quizzical brow. "If you'd stop chattering for one moment, a body could get in a word now and then. You're highly impertinent for your age."

I swallowed a laugh. "No, I ain't," I told him. Then I was at a loss once more, seeing him smile again.

He paused, considering. Then he said, "One of the mares dropped a foal last night. Come see."

My cousin kept up a constant, easy flow of talk while he steered me around the mud puddles and fended off the scolding chickens. I chose not to see any of the slaves who were working in the yard. I chose to believe my cousin and I were somewhere else, Vermont maybe. The dim vastness of the barn caught at

my heart and gave strength to the illusion. The familiar prickly scent of hay and oats and the sound of
hooves shifting on wooden planks recalled my home
to me so vividly that tears sprang to my eyes.

"It's over here," Byron said.

I followed blindly. We stopped at a stall, and I
blinked hard to see. A creamy mare, heavy and
drowsy, chewed at her hay. Beside her, a buff-coated
foal lay buckled and folded into the straw, struggling
to hold up his head and blinking uncertainly at the
world.

"His limbs are all sound," Byron said. "He's her
fourth."

I nodded. I wanted to say something, to show
Byron I wasn't the stupid ninny I must seem. "I could
help with the care of him," I finally offered. "I'd be
glad to."

"You?" Byron laughed and led me away. "If Mother even knew I'd brought you in here, she would go
into another decline." He spoke lightly, but the smile
had left his eyes. "You'll do well if you put that idea
out of your head."

"But—" I cast one last look back as we left the barn.
One of the hands, Saul, a tall man with a barrel chest,
went in the door we had left. I clamped my mouth
shut.

Byron was following my gaze. He must have apprehended the dismay that filled me every time I set eyes
on one of the slaves. He caught his hands behind his

back and regarded the sky for a moment. We were silent until he breathed a sigh.

"We are different here, Cousin," he said in a reflective voice. "Here in the South we have pursued a peculiar ideal, and to our surprise we find ourselves bound to our slaves as surely as they are bound to us. To change this now is to destroy everything we have built."

Byron looked at me, and his voice was disarmingly gentle. "It is not in my power to change it even if I would, Susannah, nor is it in yours. You must reconcile yourself. Vermont is faraway, and this is your home now."

My breath was unsteady, and I shook my head. He was wrong, I was sure. But I did not have the wit to resist his reasonable words.

"Consider also what would become of these people, ungoverned by us," he continued. "They lack in every respect the tools they need to live productively on their own. By employing them, we save them. It is to our mutual benefit. Why, even Athens, the original model of democracy, was supported by slavery. Do you read?"

I nodded mechanically, still struggling to arrange my thoughts. He overwhelmed me.

"I'll show you the library," Byron went on. "Mother discourages reading novels, as it leads to daydreaming. But, as daydreaming about democracy and the destiny of our white race are all we are allowed in Virginia, I read all the time."

I said nothing. He filled me with confusion, this handsome, courteous cousin so willing to throw in his lot with slavery. The sudden bitterness in his voice was as perplexing to me as the rest. I hardly knew what to think.

"How do you find Beth?"

"I beg your pardon?" I stammered, caught off guard yet again.

Byron was frowning at his spyglass. "Your girl—is she taking good care of you? You have no complaints?"

"No," I whispered.

"Fine." He bestowed another heroic smile upon me, and held open the front door. "I'm glad she pleases you. She's a good girl, no matter what my sister might tell you to the contrary."

I stopped on the doorsill. I had to say something.

"The library is to the right," my cousin said from behind me.

I wanted a friend with all the hope in my heart. I was bereft of parents, of familiar companions and places, and so little in my new home had presented itself to me as kind and generous. So vulnerable was I that one short hour in Byron's company could make him a hero to me, flawed as he was. You look doubtful, but I promise you, I needed so much to trust. Without a word, I preceded him.

I kept my fears hidden and allowed my cousin to show me the library. Although many of the books were history and theology and almanacs, three shelves were devoted to poetry and novels. I stood there, admiring each selection Byron offered me.

I was paging through *The Baronet's Daughter*, by Mrs. Grey, when there was a step in the hall.

"Byron?" Fidelia leaned in the doorway. As I moved from behind her brother, a different expression smoothed itself onto her face. "Ah—and dear Susannah! What have you two been about?" she asked playfully. Her eyes never left Byron's face.

He gave me a conspiratorial look. "I've undertaken to show Cousin our poor collection of books," he said, smiling at me. "Naturally, our countrymen to the North have a more scholarly tradition than we poor farmers do, but we try to keep up."

"No, no," I said, taken aback.

Fidelia touched one of her curls, and looked at the volume in my hands. "Do you read novels, Susannah?"

I looked from one to the other in bewilderment. Some other conversation seemed to be under way between them that I was not privy to. Fidelia appeared to take it very ill that I should read novels, or was it that Byron should share this occupation with me?

"I must join you," Fidelia decided. "As delicate as my constitution is, I cannot indulge myself in reading as much as I might like. But Byron often reads to me when I am too prostrated." This was said to me in a pointed tone but with a tender smile.

She lowered herself gracefully onto a chair and pressed her heart with one hand. But you would have to look far to find rosier cheeks, girls. Her infirmity was invented for her own entertainment.

"You shouldn't tire yourself, Fidelia," Byron said as he went to her side. "Let me take you into the parlor, where you can rest for a while. I'll read to you, if you like."

Fidelia raised her eyes to her brother's face. "If you really care to . . ." she said faintly.

"I would be delighted," he assured her, giving her his hand. He sent me a sardonic smile. "Excuse us, Cousin, if you would. My sister's health is an ever-present concern to me."

I did not know what to make of this exchange. I heard his voice start across the hall in a low murmur. Alone, I gazed around the library. Without Byron, it was a dim, uninviting place with hemlock branches crowding importunately outside the windows. The big house seemed very empty in spite of the voices I still heard. A dark, oppressive spirit enveloped the place, like a closing fist that shut out the light. There were half-hidden, unnameable things there that would not bear close examination. Clasping my book, I hurried up to my room.

I nearly bowled Bethlehem over as I burst through the door. She was scrubbing, as I remember, and a clod of mud from my shoe fell apart when I stepped onto the wet floor.

"I'm sorry," I said. I stooped quickly to scrape up the mud with my fingers, and our hands met as she moved to clean it, too. I withdrew my hand, and our eyes met, instead.

"I won't be but another few minutes," she said.

I hovered in the doorway, wishing I might help. "That's fine," I said foolishly. "Don't hurry on my account."

She said nothing to that but continued to scrub the bare boards. Only the downstairs rooms were covered with carpets. The upper chambers made do with woven mats and painted floorcloths. My room had only one small hooked rug with figures worked in brown, purple, and gray. It was an ugly thing, and when I stepped onto it, I was stranded upon it as a castaway would stand upon an island. Bethlehem toiled silently at my feet.

"I was going to read this book," I said, to make conversation. I held it out for her inspection, but she did not look. "I've never read this one, but I read *Ivanhoe* and enjoyed it particularly."

"Yes, miss," Bethlehem returned.

I found more enthusiasm in her answer than probably was there at first. "Did you ever read it?" I asked.

"No, miss," was her reply. She would not look up. Her shoulders moved with her vigorous efforts.

"My cousins have *Ivanhoe* in the library," I went on. I bent my knees to see her on her level. "Would you like me to get it for you?"

Bethlehem turned on me then a look of unveiled amazement. "No, miss," she said. She gathered her tools and rose, backing toward the door.

There was in her voice a tone of anger and fear that puzzled and saddened me both. I held the book behind my back because it seemed to offend her. Then I understood.

"I'm sorry. You can't read, can you?" I said. "You do know about books, don't you? You know what they are?"

She made a cautious nod. "I know what a book is for."

I was relieved, and smiled. "Well, I suppose there ain't much time for you to read, but I could teach you, if you liked it. Would you want to learn it?"

For a moment, Bethlehem stared at me. Her throat moved in a convulsive swallow. Silence stretched between us.

At last she spoke. "There's laws against it," she said flatly. "Slaves ain't supposed to know such things." Then she fumbled with the latch and hurried out.

What was I to make of that? If I had held out a handful of writhing copperheads, she could not have regarded me with more horror. But even so, I knew she had not answered my question: she did not say she wouldn't want to learn.

BETHLEHEM: I was scared! She was ignorant of our ways and eager to make a friend of me, so she held my very life in her hands. Her blunders had not yet sprung back to hurt me, but it was a question of when, not whether or not they would. So I dreaded meeting her at every turn.

And yet, she meant something. Her offer told me that there was a way for a white girl to speak to me that did not threaten or tease, scold or complain. The truth is, my own curiosity about her scared me almost as much as Susannah herself.

And then there were the books. Some of us *could* read—I knew that. Once a black preacher had visited a nearby farm and quoted Scripture until he was warned off. I knew that books could speak if a body only knew the language. They had more power than any conjure man could have. And clearest of all was this one thing: white folks could read, and white folks had the whip hand.

Still, it was worth my life not to let anyone know I wanted to know that language.

"Lizer," I said when I saw her in the yard.

She had a chicken under her arm, and it glared at me like a devil was inside it. "Catch me that red one," Lizer said.

I knew from her voice she was stretched for time. Someone wanted something *now*, a stewed chicken or some pot liquor, and didn't mind letting Lizer know it. So I held my peace for a while.

I stalked the red hen while Lizer headed toward the kitchen. It knew something was going to happen, saw I wasn't tossing out greens or eggshells. A suspicious cluck squeezed through that bird, and it strutted carefully, carefully, keeping one eye cocked at me. If I had time, I would have tried trancing it, but I had no patience for a long chase and I grabbed the hen before it had time to get alarmed. It pecked me hard, but I couldn't blame it. I'd have pecked, too, if I could.

Lizer had already chopped the head off the first chicken. Its eye still stared up at me from the dust beside the block. The body was jerking and dripping from Lizer's hand.

"Lizer," I began again. "Did you ever want to learn reading?"

She sniffed, and curled her lip at the lump of feathers she held by the feet. "What do I want with reading?" she asked in disgust, putting the body aside. "Messing with buckra's ways only gets me more trouble than I got already."

My chicken pecked me again. "But wouldn't it be a good thing?" I pressed.

"Don't you go on about that," Lizer said angrily. "Don't you pester me about it any. Give me that hen."

I held it tighter, my throat dry. "But if a body knew reading, he could go somewheres and know what was what." The chicken jabbed at me good and hard, and I yelped.

"Give me that bird!" Lizer snapped, yanking it from me and slapping it onto the block. In one motion, she raised her hatchet and brought it down. The head landed in the dirt next to the other, blinking in furious surprise.

I nursed my hand and stared at the heads.

"Now get these birds cleaned," Lizer said. Her voice was shaking. "I got a lot to do."

Her meaning was clear enough. Slaves messing with such things would only end up with misery, end up blinking and gaping when somebody swiped their heads off. I wondered if it could be worth the trouble.

And then I saw Byron idling along, saw him catch sight of me and steer a course in my direction. It wouldn't be long before he tired of that courting game and wanted something more. And I thought, Dear Lord, how much worse will it get?

1·8·9·6

When Gran and I got to our room in the Victoria Hotel later, Gran lay right down to rest. The long train ride and the talk at Bethlehem's had worn us both out.

But I was restless. Terrible, bitter pictures filled my imagination. I wanted to protect the young girl that was my grandmother, but I had no way to do it. To make my emotions even more confused, I still chafed at the unfair treatment I felt I had received in Bethlehem's room. I knelt on a chair to twitch the curtain aside and looked down on the street. The gas lamps were coming on, glowing feebly through the rain. Carriage wheels hissed through puddles.

"Are you hungry?" Gran asked softly from the bed.

"No, ma'am."

The room was silent with closing darkness. Frowning hard, I rubbed the carvings on the chair back and pressed in a dent with my thumbnail. I made another, and another, knowing how wrong I was to mar it, until I had impressed a small "M" on the dark wood. I covered it with my hand.

"Gran?"

"Yes, Mary."

"Did you teach her to read?"

"Yes."

"Why?" I asked. "You might have been punished. Wasn't it against the law?"

She sighed. "Yes, it was. Ignorance is a heavy chain, and it works well. Teaching a Negro to read was a kind of treason, I suppose."

"But how could you break the law?"

"Mary." Gran raised herself on her elbow and looked at me gravely. "I was lonely."

I turned my face back to the window. My heart was full, but I could not explain what filled it. I saw a lack in me that was not there before we arrived in Toronto. It was unfair, all of it, and too much for me. I started to cry.

"I want to go home," I choked. "I hate it here!"

Gran was at my side but did not touch me. "I'm sorry."

A silence opened up between us, leaving a wide, cold space. I expected her to take me in her arms and tell me we could leave. But she did not.

"You are not a child any longer, Mary."

I caught my breath and pleated the fabric of my dress between my fingers. Only that morning I had thought myself quite dignified and mature, traveling in the world. Now I was ridiculous and vain in my own eyes.

"Yes, ma'am," I whispered.

Then Gran laid a hand on my head, and the cold space closed up again. "I wanted you to come with me, my dear. I thought you could share this with me. . . ." She gazed through the window, too, and sighed deeply.

There was a sadness in her that made me sorry, but confused as well. The story was sad, but yet there we all were. Clearly, she and Bethlehem had both succeeded in leaving that bad place behind. All had turned out for the best, or so it seemed.

"I am glad you wanted me to come with you, Gran," I said.

She smiled suddenly and drew me near. "It has been a long day, hasn't it? You have been very patient. I didn't mean for this to hurt you, Mary."

With a sigh, I leaned my head against her side and breathed in the faint rose scent that touched all her clothes. I had a strong sense of her being *there*, real, my grandmother. But perhaps she was not the woman I thought I knew.

The following morning, we stopped at a grocer's for cheese, bread, and apples to take to Bethlehem's rooms. When we arrived, I could see right off that Bethlehem's illness had driven her hard during the night: her skin had an ashy tone to it, and her movements had lost their previous briskness. Free also looked tired and anxious, and I noticed that the bed behind its discreet screen was unmade, the covers askew, as though hurriedly flung back. But Bethlehem dismissed Gran's expressions of concern and merely asked if we were all ready to continue with the story.

"Mary wants to know why I was foolish enough to teach a slave to read," Gran said.

Bethlehem turned her thoughtful gaze on me, but before she could speak, Free scraped back her chair.

"It couldn't have hurt you," she said with some scorn, looking coldly at my grandmother. "But it could have gotten Miss Reid a whipping."

I was ready to come to Gran's defense in an instant. "It was still kindly meant," I retorted, unwilling for anyone to misunderstand my grandmother's goodness and generosity. "There was a law against it. She wouldn't have broken that idly. And there was surely a risk to her in doing so."

Free clenched her jaw, stared at me, and then looked at Bethlehem. "Not half the risk you took. They could have whipped you or put you in leg irons. I know that. Back in slavery days, we could get beaten to death for taking eggs."

"That's true," Bethlehem agreed in even tones.

Free still faced her with a challenge. "They beat you, didn't they? Didn't that Mass Reid whip you? Isn't that why you ran off when you did?"

Nobody spoke. I looked swiftly from Gran to Bethlehem, but both were pensive, quiet. Free was breathing hard, and I was shocked that such a storm of outrage could spring up so abruptly. I wished the rain would stop and release us from its oppressive shadow. I ached for sunlight and blue sky.

Then Bethlehem moved one shoulder in a curious, negating motion. She looked at her hands and moved them apart. "He never did beat me, no."

A look of hurt and angry bewilderment came into Free's eyes at that. I can hardly describe the sequence of thoughts that went through my mind as I looked at her then. I saw her as the embodiment of the young Bethlehem, with that same bewildered look on her face. In the girl Bethlehem's expression, I saw a picture of rebellious, sorrowful disbelief that things were as they were: that she could be pursued relentlessly by a young white man; that she could be pinched and slapped and subjected to every petty indignity Fidelia could dream up; that her master could value her as he would a horse or cow, and could as readily dispose of her; that her life was a sum of meanness, degradation, and hateful dependency; that she was, in short, a slave, and utterly powerless to change her lot. Life for her could be no worse. That was reason enough to run away.

Gran broke the silence. "I won't make excuses for being reckless," she told Free. "I simply did not believe in my heart that teaching Bethlehem to read was dangerous. I was ignorant, and also, I wanted occupation."

I was lonely. The words she had spoken last night remained unsaid. I heard an echo of them but did not bring them up.

"Let me try to explain something," Gran said. She adjusted her spectacles and paused. "You live here in the city, Free, and there are people all around you."

Free looked as though she would speak, but seemed to change her mind. She looked down, stonefaced, while Gran continued.

"It is commonplace to know what all the others about you know. But in the South, especially then, farms were far apart. For weeks at a time, we saw no neighbors unless we traveled into town for Sunday service. A farm is an isolated thing, and the people on it have only one another for their friends or enemies. There was little news, and only our own amusements."

"A farm surely is a dangerous place," Bethlehem summed up. She covered her eyes with one hand, remembering.

I tried to imagine the Reids' farm as Gran described it, and could not. Free picked up a book and toyed with the cover.

"Would you rather she never taught me?" Bethlehem asked Free in an amused voice. She tapped her pupil's shoulder and waited for some look from her. At last, Free gave Bethlehem a grudging smile. "After all,

I noticed you enjoying the gift of reading I passed on to *you*. Maybe not every homeless child wants to be raised by a teacher, but you surely do eat it like honey."

"Yes, but—" Free sighed.

"Let me try to justify myself a bit better," Gran said. "Let me see if I can explain why instead of finding something else to occupy myself, I kept encouraging Bethlehem to learn her letters."

"Pestering is more like it," Bethlehem said under her breath. She was trying not to smile.

Gran looked to the ceiling and shook her head. "Oh, my Lord. Now who's being stubborn?"

Bethlehem laughed. "Go on. You just try to make these girls see things a little clearer."

I picked up the pen eagerly.

SPRING
1·8·5·5

SUSANNAH: I know it may seem peculiar that I did not try harder to make a friend of Fidelia or Byron, but would choose instead to seek out a black slave girl. I can only say that Fidelia and I had a natural antipathy toward each other that was evident from the first, and we made no pretense of love. She was peevish, indolent, and vain, or seemed so to me then. Now, I suppose she was lonely and raised to believe she was made of finer stuff than everyone around her. And of course, her strong affection for Byron made any newcomer an instant rival.

It was perhaps for this reason as well that Byron could not relieve my loneliness. The more attention he paid to me, the more aversion Fidelia displayed. And for all his charm, there was a weakness in Byron that I was not old enough to forgive: he was an apologist for slavery. I avoided him finally. And although young ladies at that time were discouraged from idleness, my aunt took very little notice of me. Whenever she hap-

pened upon me, she acted rather surprised, and then
set me to some small domestic task, such as copying
out recipes, counting stores, or making lace for the
missionaries. I was thus very much alone.

If I had been given a puppy or a weakling lamb to
raise up, I might not have noticed Bethlehem to the
extent that I did. As it was, I blush to tell you that I
saw her as a project, and I was relentless in trying to
reach her.

"Will you hand me my Bible?" I asked her one
morning, not long after I arrived. I pointed deliber-
ately at the table, on which lay two books.

Bethlehem picked up both of them, but I shook my
head. "It's the one with the *B* on it. See there?" I
went to her side and traced the *B* in Bible with my
finger. "It's the same letter that starts your name,
Beth."

"The same?" she asked me. "My name is the same
as the Bible?"

I was elated at this small interest in her. "Just the
first letter. All the different words are made up of
letters—like a recipe for bread or cake. The letters are
the ingredients, but they go in order."

Bethlehem regarded the two books in her hand.
She seemed to struggle with this notion. After a moment, she pressed her lips firmly together and put
both books into my hands.

"I wouldn't know about that, miss," she said. She
started to leave.

"Wait!" I let the Bible fall open where it would and read the first verses my eyes came upon.

" 'For the Lord is a great God, and a great King above all gods. In his hand are the deep places of the earth: the strength of the hills is his also. The sea is his, and he made it: and his hands formed the dry land.' "

I looked up when I had finished it. Bethlehem eyed the book in my hands.

"Ain't it pretty?" I asked her.

"Bible says that?" Bethlehem said. Some great emotion was working in her: her hands clenched each other violently. "You can read the Bible?"

"I can read any old book, as long as it's in American," I said, and held it out to her.

Like one hypnotized, Bethlehem returned to my side and looked at the mysterious words on the page. I held my breath, for the truth is, I did not know if she could learn it. It was widely believed back then that the Negro was an inferior race of slow intelligence.

Then she pointed to the word "Behold."

"Is that another one?" she asked. "Like Bible and Beth?"

"Yes!" I laughed, quite proud of what I had done.

We looked at each other for a triumphant moment. Then the veil came between us again, and Bethlehem dropped her gaze. "I got no use for books and such, miss," she said in a strained voice.

I let her go, but I resolved on proving to her that

learning her letters was useful. I knew I would win the case.

Our lessons thus began. I rejoiced in having such a worthy task, and the secrecy required lent our operations a delightful sense of adventure to me. Also, I was conscious of a true pleasure as her proficiency grew. I fancied myself quite a good teacher. Her time was constrained and our lessons very short and irregular. For her part, Bethlehem showed a maddening mix of eagerness and hesitancy, and throughout she demonstrated a deference to me that was both flattering and vexing. Whenever I would spontaneously clasp her hand in congratulation, she withdrew it and soon recalled a job she had to do.

There were many times when I forgot her color, and thought of her as my equal. Then, the juxtaposition of our faces in the mirror, or of our two hands side by side, would recall me. I am ashamed to say that I wished fervently she could have been white. And, yes, you are certainly right to be indignant to hear me admit it.

All the while, the habit of life was reasserting itself in me. The loss I felt for my parents had subsided to a low bass note accompanying my daily routine; sometimes, indeed, it was not audible at all. But not because I was more reconciled to my new situation. It never felt like home. I still pined for Vermont, although at first it was a hopeless wish.

At this time, however, I began reading through Andersen's *Danish Storybook*. I wept over the sad tales of orphans, and their griefs acutely recalled my own. But I was also inspired by those small heroes and heroines who wandered through snow and ice all alone: here, I thought, was a lesson in self-reliance I might follow. The fact that they commonly met with misfortune or death was inconsequential. The notion of running away began to take shape in my breast.

BETHLEHEM: As you can see, Susannah saw our lessons as a game. Keeping such a dangerous secret made her happy and lightened her cares. I was sure that once she tired of it, the secret would come out, and I expected a terrible punishment. Yet I could not turn away from what she held out in her skinny hand. It was a perilous gift. No wonder she thought I was ignorant and superstitious. Maybe I was.

One day, Miz Reid sent me to the library to fetch a shawl she had left there. The books on the shelves were like live things: I could feel them behind me, waiting to open their mouths and speak to me. This fear grew so strong that I dared not turn around. For several moments, I held my breath, sure the books would make me betray myself. I had caught a few words without even trying: *World, Homer, Year*. Turn around, and there would be even more, like a chorus of tar-colored crows, fighting to see which one could croak the loudest. At last, I shut my eyes and ran out of the room.

"What ails you?" Miz Reid asked when I gave her the shawl.

"Nothing, Miz Reid." There was a book on the table beside her in the parlor. I found myself staring at it: *Satan, Morals, Church*. I made my face a blank.

There were circulars and periodicals as well: *Female Complaint, Home, Newest Style*. Words jumped at me from everywhere.

"Nothing?" Miz Reid was a foolish woman in many ways, but she had sharp eyes when she chose to look. She was looking at me hard, now. "You act as though you had seen a ghost," she said.

I grabbed the explanation I knew would please her. "I did, Miz Reid!" I said, widening my eyes and fidgeting with my apron. "I saw a spirit in the liberry."

She colored up. "You darkies are so credulous," she exclaimed. "Go tell Lizer I'll take supper in my room. I'm not well at all."

I hied out of there. Unluckily, I ran into Byron in the hallway.

"Steady, Beth!" He laughed, catching my arm. He was holding the spyglass he set such store by and set it down carefully on the sideboard. "Where are you rushing to?"

"A chore for your mama," I told him. I pulled away, but he held my arm tight. "I got to go."

He was smiling his same old honey smile. Oh, he was handsome, handsome. "Your kerchief is askew. Let me put it right."

I could not move while he knotted it at my throat. He let his hands rest against my dress as he did this, and he still smiled, even in his eyes. I held my breath to keep from breathing in the smell of him.

"Byron! Is that you?"

He started. "Yes, Mother. Get on your way," he said to me before he walked into the parlor.

I stood quiet a moment. Then I picked up his spyglass and turned it over in my hands. It was still warm from his touch, solid yellow brass. I went down the hall, onto the porch, and brought the wide end of the spyglass down on the boot scraper. When I saw the sparkle like bits of ice on the floor, I took a long, deep breath. Then I put Byron's toy back on the sideboard again and came away.

SUSANNAH: Well, my Lord! I always wondered what had happened to that spyglass. I can tell you I felt like breaking some of Fidelia's things when she was particularly irritating. I never dared, though. Mostly I just hid in my room when I was that vexed. But I do remember the day that spyglass turned up broken. Byron surely was put out. I thought he'd ask me what I knew, but he never did.

Spring was well along by that time. The farm was run entirely by the industry of the slaves, and there was little for young ladies, such as Fidelia and myself, to do but improve ourselves, as the saying was. Fidelia improved herself by studying dress styles in *Godey's* and complaining that hers were not *à la mode*. I improved myself by planning my escape.

I spent a great deal of time in my room. Ostensibly, I was resting. Resting was much encouraged, as a delicate constitution in a young woman was considered genteel. Had my aunt and uncle known that I took my rest with Sir Walter Scott, Mr. Defoe, and Mr. Poe, they would have been appalled. In young ladies, reading fiction could only encourage idle reveries. But my reveries were far from being idle. They were active and purposeful to an inspiring degree.

As an antidote to my rests, I took frequent airings. When in sight of the house, I walked decorously, but once I gained the woods I ran and leaped like a wild thing. Needless to say, Bethlehem always chaperoned. She looked stunned the first time I climbed a tree, but then I saw her smile behind her hand.

"I have an idea, Beth," I told her on a warm day in late May. We were bathing our feet in the stream that ran a mile or so from the farm. "I need you to help me through with it."

As always, Bethlehem was the spirit of acquiescence. She nodded. "Yes, miss."

I busied myself peeling a stick. "Beth, I want to go

back to Vermont, but I have a notion my uncle would sooner bark like a dog in church than let me."

I saw her lips twitch before she turned away. "Yes, miss," she said.

"So I must steal away," I went on. "It's a heavy secret. Don't tell a soul, not Lizer, not anybody. I am in bitter earnest on this."

Bethlehem shook her head. She was retying her scarf, so I could not read her expression. But I fancied she listened with a new intensity.

The romantical stories I had read were one riotous stew in my mind. From it, I had only to pluck the proper tactics.

"First of all, I shall disguise myself as a boy. I'm glad I'm still small."

Bethlehem glanced at my figure and then at her own, which was not so girlish as mine but still immature. She was nearly as slender as I was.

I lay back on my elbows in the weeds and contemplated the sky. "I'll cut my hair short and find some of Byron's old clothes. Then I'll set off up the river."

The river. The Shenandoah snakes along at the foot of the western slopes in the Blue Ridge, up past Front Royal to join the Potomac at Harper's Ferry. That town and the name of John Brown were not yet infamous in Virginia, but would be within five years. You've read, I'm sure, of the slave rebellion that took place there in 1859. John Brown was a fervent abolitionist but, alas, a terrible general, and Robert E. Lee rounded up that desperate small army in only a day. That slaves would rise up in arms against the masters came as a grievous shock to the South, for some reason. Some say the Civil War really started there where the Shenandoah meets the Potomac, in Harper's Ferry, with poor John Brown. But of course, this had not yet happened.

The very stream by which we sat wound down to join the Shenandoah: my plan was simply to follow it, and head north. Beyond were Maryland, Pennsylvania, New York, and Vermont. It sounded simple. Four states to pass through, and on the map Maryland was nothing but a crooked arm poked between two of them. I anticipated a journey of some five to six weeks, assuming some kindly travelers would let me ride some stages of the way.

I had no doubt but that I could manage it. The weather would be fair and mild, I was accustomed to walking, and I knew how to trap and skin small game. Success needed only the will to push on, and I had an abundance of that.

"I'll have to contrive somehow to lay a false trail," I continued. "That is one way you can help me the most. What do you say?" I pressed Bethlehem. "Will you help me carry it through? Only help me to get ready, and then deny you know anything once I'm away."

I little thought at the time what risk I was putting her to. My imagination could compass only my own situation.

She was silent, frowning at the dazzle of light on the stream. To my eyes, she look distressed. I sat up and put one hand on her arm.

"I'm sorry we won't continue our lessons," I told her. "But you know all the letters now, and I think you can get on by yourself."

"Where will you go?" she brought out at last.

I closed my eyes and saw it: the rotten-sweet apples on the ground, the wafer of ice on a puddle in October, Old Monk dragging a plow through dark and stony earth.

"Home," I whispered.

"Home."

Bethlehem's voice was an echo, so faint I might have imagined it from my own longing.

I clutched her arm again in a passion of urgency. "Won't you help me?"

She looked down at my hand on her arm and nodded. "Yes, miss."

I happily lay back again and let my thoughts roam. Before August was concluded, I felt sure, I would be fishing in the Battenkill with my old childhood friend Nat once more.

All difficulties paled beside this one sure fact. I had only to make my preparations.

1·8·9·6

I was frankly astonished by Gran's words. My demure, ladylike grandmother spoke so casually about skinning game, masquerading as a boy! I reread the last few words I had taken down and shook my head.

"I shock you, don't I?" Gran laughed.

I was about to agree when I saw the skeptical smile on Free's lips and changed my mind. "I know you are very resourceful, Gran," I demurred.

"I certainly regarded Bethlehem as a resource," Gran said. "How careless and unconsidering I was."

"There wasn't too much danger," Bethlehem said. "We did have the run of the place, and white master couldn't always be checking up. I knew I could manage those things fine. I thought you were crazy, though," she added with a rich, throaty chuckle.

All three of them laughed, and I felt somewhat at a loss. This angered me. Normally, I was very much at home wherever I went, but since arriving in Toronto everything I said and did seemed wrong. Gran covered my hand with hers.

"I underestimated by a bit," she said, smiling merrily.

"Did you do it the way you planned it?" I asked. I was impatient.

Gran folded her spectacles. "I became the very model of stealth. I did indeed find some britches and other clothes of Byron's. I compelled Bethlehem to steal me a knife and some phosphorous matches from the kitchen, and I petitioned Uncle to be allowed one ladylike ride each day."

I stared again, horrified. "You were going to steal a *horse*?"

"I was determined to get home," Gran replied evenly. "I made no attempt to justify my actions. I gave no thought to any consideration."

This was an irreverent side to my grandmother I had not imagined.

"If I did, I also believed that I was in a state of sin," Gran added. "Even living under a minister's roof— especially under *that* minister's roof—couldn't atone for that sin. Any route to leave it was sanctified."

"Stealing from a man like that isn't stealing anyhow," Free announced.

"Slaves thought that, you can be sure," Bethlehem said. "Lizer used to say, if she took some eggs for herself, then Master still had them since he still had her." She twined her fingers. "Of course, for Susannah, it was different. She *was* stealing."

Gran arched her eyebrows. "Why was it stealing for me but not stealing for you?"

Bethlehem looked at her for a moment. "You know why. The situation was different."

"Perhaps, but only by degree," Gran countered.

"I'm not sure I understand you."

There was a stillness in the small room. Free and I both felt it, and we shared a quick, anxious glance.

"I owned nothing, my activity and my future were strictly proscribed, I was expected to do my uncle's bidding or suffer the consequences," Gran said. Her voice shook.

"But you were free," Bethlehem said.

Gran made a fist. "I was not free! I was a girl and an orphan! My uncle might have used me as hard as any slave, and I should have had no recourse! For what other reason did I run away?"

"You wanted to go home," I reminded her, frightened by her passion.

Gran finally looked away from Bethlehem and noticed me. She drew breath. "Yes." She sighed. "I wanted to go home."

Free got up then and offered to make tea. We were all glad for a distraction and busily cleared space on the small table among the papers and inkwell.

My imagination did not rest, however. I tried to picture my grandmother staying at her uncle's farm: she might have grown self-absorbed like her aunt, spiteful and violent like Fidelia, or apologetic like

Byron. Her uncle remained the cipher in this story. How like him she might have become, I can't say. He was one who had bought and sold other human beings. The prospect of finding that within one's own character must have been chilling.

Of course, I doubt that my grandmother had formed these thoughts to herself. Perhaps she only knew she dreaded living there too long. One day she might beat her maid for some imagined insult, and she would be lost.

"I'll take a turn writing next," Free offered when she came back to the table. She gave me a tentative smile.

"Thank you." I flexed my hand and glanced quickly at Gran and Bethlehem.

My grandmother's hand trembled very slightly as she raised her teacup. Bethlehem must have noticed it, too, because she touched Gran's arm gently.

"You're doing a fine job telling the story, Sue," she said. "I hardly have to put in my two cents at all."

"You have more than two cents invested in this story," Gran returned with a shaky smile. She sipped her tea. "Quite a bit more."

SPRING
1·8·5·5

BETHLEHEM: Susannah's plans to run away meant nothing to me at first. She could make these ideas to lighten her cares, but there were no ideas I could make at all. One day, I knew, she would simply be gone, and life on the farm would go on as it had before I ever heard her name. Slaves made few attachments that didn't get broken: our lives were cheap, and love even cheaper. I knew better than to allow myself any tender feelings for that girl.

One day we were in her room. She was looking over my shoulder to watch me wade through some verses in the Bible, when she broke in.

"I found a map," she whispered, her eyes kindling. "I daren't draw my road on it, but I want to show you."

With a hasty look at the closed door, she pulled a large book from under her bed. She opened it up. I hated to stop my own reading, but she was strong in the way of convincing.

"This is a picture of this country. Here is where we are," she said, pointing to a black spot with one finger. "And this is where I aim to go."

I followed along, across the patches of yellow, pink, and dusty blue, not knowing what distances these were. Maps were mute and shut to me. But right above the yellowy shape where her finger stopped was a black line and a wide clear space with no marks or writing.

"What is that?" I asked, touching that emptiness.

She waved her hand. "Oh, that's just Canada up there."

Everything in me stopped to listen—my breath, my blood, my heart. I pressed my hand down to keep her from seeing it shake. My fingers spread out across Canada. "What is it?"

"Another country," she said. "The whole world ain't the United States of America, you know. Vermont goes right up to it. Look, see this line here? It's the Battenkill River. It's real pretty."

"Yes." I was looking at that wide white space. The Promised Land wasn't just a story slaves had. It might be real. It was in one of buckra's books.

"Beth, you're smudging this page, now," Susannah went on, pushing my hand away. "I just wanted you to know where I'm going."

That wide white space didn't have any of the lines or shapes on it that the rest of the map had. Was it only an emptiness where the land stopped? Was it a silent nothing? Could that be any worse than the place I was in? And Susannah's place, her Vermont, was right by it: perhaps there was a kinship there; perhaps Vermont was a good place, too.

I had never thought of running until Susannah put it in my head. Before that, the dull, same old sameness of my days was like a dose of laudanum: nothing changed; nothing happened. I was no way resigned to my life, but neither was I desperate. Besides, the whispers about runaways were tales of panic in the woods, dogs, recapture, chains. There was a line that needed stepping over to face those things. I needed something to push me. What started to push was a skinny white girl with foolish ideas but a strong power of wanting.

And Susannah's path lay along the road to Canada. It was something for me to think on.

Mass Reid took a newspaper from town regularly. When he had done with them, they turned up in the kitchen for laying fires or wrapping food. When anyone was about, even Lizer, I was as blind to the printed words as a cat.

But once I knew how, I could not stop myself from reading when I was alone. Two days after Susannah showed me her map, I saw a notice. I spelled it out bit by bit.

WARNING!

ILLEGAL TRAFFICKERS IN STOLEN SLAVES.

———◦———

Three Male Slaves, Property of Silas Burgoyne
of This City, Valued at $400 ea., Stolen by
Rogues.
Information Leading to Their Recapture Will Be
Rewarded.

In slavery days, news passed like a breeze between
slave and slave, cabin and cabin, farm and farm. We all
knew that down South, deep South, a body could die
in cane fields and rice fields. Being sold to a master
from the deep South was a terrible fear in us upper
South slaves. Traffic in stolen slaves was traffic to
Alabama, Louisiana, and Florida, where field hands
perished quickly and needed constant replacement.

So finding out such traffickers were nearby put me
in a cold sweat. Lizer came into the kitchen then and
found me staring.

"What got you, child?" she asked. "Somebody put
the eye on you?"

I could not tell her what I knew. I could not tell her
I had read it.

"No, ma'am," I whispered. I touched a flame to the
paper and watched it curl.

But while the burn flowed across the newsprint, I
had another idea that burned me as hot as the paper: a
slave who disappeared when such folk were nearby was
not thought a runaway. And a body that went looking
for such a missing slave would start looking south.

SUSANNAH: All I wanted now was a story to cover my tracks. Being kidnapped by Indians struck me as a likely tale, but since the Cherokees had been pushed out to Oklahoma in 1838, I doubted anybody would credit it. There were some Indians left in the vicinity, but they were no more likely to steal a white girl than run for governor of Virginia. There were plenty of bears around still, and I finally hit on that as my sorry fate. Yes, I know. It was certainly the most absurd foolishness, but I resolved I would be eaten by bears.

The thought gave me a wonderful sense of relief, since now all I had to do was go, and somehow leave a trail to suggest I had been carried off. But it made me melancholic as well. Would anybody be sorry to hear I had suffered such a horrible death? Fidelia might give a fastidious shudder and possibly swoon if Byron were nearby to catch her. My aunt would no doubt put it all down to God's will and indulge in a fit of praying. My uncle might be secretly relieved he had one less mouth to feed.

But what of Byron? I went to seek him out, hoping to gauge his reaction to my imminent death. It was twilight, and the house was quiet. Uncle was in town, and Fidelia was playing some insipid airs on the forte-piano for my aunt. Byron was nowhere to be found.

So I thought to find Bethlehem, and see if she had

all that I needed. In the summer kitchen, Lizer said she knew nothing of her whereabouts. I tramped outside, kicking at pebbles. Bethlehem's cabin was empty and dark, with a smell of woodsmoke and bacon lingering. Vexed, I wandered off toward the paddocks for a look at the horses. They moved slowly along, grazing into the night. An owl hooted off in the woods. I plucked a weed and batted the air with it, wandering aimlessly. I lifted my skirts and saw my stockings shining white in the blue light. Raising first one foot and then the other to see the flash of my stockings, I felt loose, unanchored: soon I would be gone. The world felt immense, revolving in the universe with small Susannah McKnight clinging to it.

I passed the barn, and my cousin's voice reached me.

"Now, don't be so stubborn."

There was a low murmur in reply. I stepped nearer the barn, into its shadow. I did not mean to be eavesdropping, which I had always deemed a low, dishonorable trick. I intended to make my presence known the next moment. But then I recognized Bethlehem's voice and stopped in confusion. What were Byron and Bethlehem doing, arguing in the barn at dusk?

"I won't do it," she said.

"I could make you. You know that."

"I know it."

"But I don't force you, you see. And I won't, unless

you keep putting on these foolish impostures. This play of modesty in you is absurd."

I could not hear Bethlehem's answer. My face burned, although I did not rightly know what they were discussing. I heard my cousin say something unintelligible, and there was a scuffle. He cried out in pain and surprise.

"You shouldn't have done that," he said, his voice low and controlled.

His footsteps came near the door, and I pressed myself into the shadow. As he strode away from me to the house, I found myself trembling.

Bethlehem walked out the door, her head bent.

"Did you hit him?" I gasped, unable to stop myself.

She turned around. In the failing light, her face was difficult to see. She didn't answer me.

"How dare you?" I said. I was shaking from head to foot. "How dare you strike him!"

When she still did not answer, I shamed myself by bursting into tears. "I hate it here!" I sobbed. Bethlehem moved not a muscle, and I stepped toward her with my hand raised to slap her face. She did not flinch.

"What did he want?" I whispered, trying to see her.

"Something I won't give."

I dropped my hand. Such a feeling of weariness came over me I wanted to curl up on the ground and close my eyes to the world. It wasn't Bethlehem I wanted to strike at all, but some other terrible thing. I had never hit even an animal before, but I had almost cracked Bethlehem across her mouth, looking for blood. That was an evil, evil impulse and made me wish to die.

"Beth, I have to leave tomorrow. Tomorrow."

I leaned my head back and stared at the stars. They could not be the same stars that wheeled above New England. How could they be? How could this be the same world? Bats careened above me, jagged particles of night. My mind was a blank.

"I'm going with you."

I was still staring at the stars, the bats like winks across my vision. Slowly, I heard in my head what Bethlehem had just spoken out loud. "What?"

Bethlehem drew a shuddering breath. I realized she was crying, or trying not to. "I can help you if you help me."

"But—"

"They'll think we got stolen by those slave-stealing men," she whispered. "I saw it in a news sheet."

My mind spun. What she was suggesting was—I couldn't think, but I rebelled inwardly. She belonged to my uncle. Did she have this outrageous notion because of something she had read, something I had taught her to read? I was responsible. I had never looked for this. I had started something going that I wasn't ready to acknowledge, and it frightened me. You see, I was young, and didn't want to confront the hard side to my decisions.

"Beth. You can't." We stared at each other. All I could see of her were her eyes. She looked down at the ground.

What if she were to betray me? I wondered then. Once alert my uncle, and I would never have another chance. I considered carefully. To my way of thinking, I had already begun my journey and must not halt or falter.

"Very well. We'll go tomorrow."

She raised her eyes finally and looked at me. Then she nodded once and turned away.

———

BETHLEHEM: I swear, my knees were so weak I could hardly hold myself up. But I walked straight to my cabin before my legs gave out. I rested my forehead against the door and breathed deeply. My whole body began to shake like a demon, so hard that my teeth clacked and I ended up retching in the fireplace.

I kneeled in the ashes some time. Any minute, they would storm in and take me away, sell me south or worse. I would never have another chance to let such craziness pass my lips.

But nobody came. The dogs did not bark; no lights shone anywhere. Finally I dippered up some water to rinse my mouth. I was used to finding things in the dark, and my hands came to the bundle of Susannah's things: matches, knife, boy's clothes, boots. Tonight I would find clothes for myself, and tomorrow I would leave with Susannah.

With Susannah.

Again I found myself trembling, but I clutched the bundle and hurried outside for a breath of air. Above me, the stars spread out in their multitudes like a strew of cornmeal across a table, like a host of angels crossing River Jordan.

"Dear King Jesus," I whispered. "Help this child."

A breeze came up and parted the branches to my left. There I saw the dipper, the gourd in the sky pointing to the North Star. I had no notion how far away Vermont was, but it was North and that was where I needed to go. I was going to get there with a knife, some matches, and a white girl dressed as a boy.

SUSANNAH: I awoke early the next morning, filled with hope. The prospect of leaving that hated place overcame the apprehensiveness I felt about taking Bethlehem along with me. I took my small shears from my sewing box, rolled them in a handkerchief, and put them in my pocket. It was one thing I could do to feel I was forwarding my plan. Then I sat by the window to watch the sun come up.

In the three months I had been in Virginia, I had started each day in this manner. I don't know why the first stirrings on the farm always made me so lonesome, but they did. I saw the hounds loping around, finding new smells, the horses ambling in the paddocks cropping grass, and Monday creaking his slow, weary way past the cabins. Certainly I was not sorry to be seeing the last of my uncle's farm, but that spreading bounty was a fine prospect to look on in the morning. When Bethlehem walked out her door, I stood up, prickly with anticipation.

My scheme was still misty and shapeless. But all there was to do was get up and leave. Bethlehem and I would saddle the pony I always rode, and we would simply go. At some remote spot, I would transform myself into a boy. Beyond that, I knew only to strike north until we hit Vermont. What else was there to know? My lonesome feeling ebbed as the dawn spread across the horizon to the east and north, lighting my way.

"Morning, Miz Susannah," Bethlehem whispered to me as she entered my room.

I was smiling, but trying not to. I wanted her to know I was conscious of the gravity of our plan. Then I spoiled the effect by letting out a gasp.

"We're going!" I laughed breathlessly. I whirled around with my arms wide.

Bethlehem stiffened. Then she inclined her head toward the door in a listening posture. The house was still sleeping around us.

"Don't be so nervous," I teased her, running over to give her arm a shake. "Nothing will go wrong."

I chattered on, though careful to keep my voice low. Bethlehem winced at my every outburst, and her anxiousness began to put a damper on my spirits. It annoyed me that she would be so fearful when such an adventure loomed before us. She was the very pattern of gloom. After only a few minutes, she broke in.

"Let's us go outside, miss," she begged, her eyes shifting from side to side.

I nodded. "Very well. Let's not dawdle anymore." I took one last look at my small room. I wouldn't miss it at all, but the pile of books on the table afforded me a twinge of regret. There was no reason to take books along on a morning ride, so I had to leave them behind. Nothing must appear out of the ordinary to betray us.

Bethlehem was tugging on my arm all the while, and I finally shook her loose. "I'm coming!" I told her. "Don't worry at me like that."

We hurried down the stairs and out to the barn. Monday was tramping back from the hog pens with a bucket in each hand.

"Fine morning for a ride," he said. "Nice and cool."

Bethlehem faltered and stopped. A stricken look came into her face as she tried to speak to him. I held my breath: one signal that we were escaping would spell disaster. Did she appreciate that fact? I widened my eyes at her, but she saw only old Monday.

"How's your misery this morning, Monday?" she said finally.

He shook his head slowly and eased his back. "It's bad. It's mighty bad today, Beth."

Bethlehem's throat worked. Her eyes looked huge. "Take some of that liniment Lizer went and made for you," she whispered.

"I think I will. Soon's I get done with the hogs," he replied. He picked up his bucket again and resumed his slow progress across the yard.

"Come on if you're coming," I warned her. I didn't know what gave her so much trouble in leaving. There was nothing for her there, I thought. She was an orphan the same as I.

She drew a breath. "I'm coming."

Then we went into the barn, saddled my pony, and trotted quickly off the farm.

BETHLEHEM: There was nothing for me there, it's true, and every reason to run away. But not being able to say a good-bye to that old Monday—or any of the others—nearly cracked my heart open. I wanted to choke Susannah for rushing me so, but there was nothing I could have said in any case. She was as giddy as a girl on a Sunday picnic, and trying to look solemn all the while.

"Where did you hide our things?" she asked as we jogged along. She seemed not to notice my deep silence. "Are we out of view yet? Don't turn around to look. You'll love Vermont, Beth. They don't have slavery up there, so you'll be free. Why, you're free already—don't you know it?"

We were riding on a track through pine trees, where the rusty needles were thick under the pony's hooves. Sunlight sliced down between the trees, and mist dropped from withery old branches. No matter how Susannah babbled, I couldn't hear her through the wet and heavy silence around us. There was a part of me still left behind, but it was stretching thinner and thinner the farther we went. Any minute I knew it would snap like a thread. I could see it stretching and stretching out behind me; the thinness of it began to terrify my heart. I closed my eyes tight shut and tried to see something else, something wide and fine.

"Where's our things?" Susannah asked.

We were at the stream by then. The pony turned and lazied up along it. I touched Susannah's shoulder. "Here," I said when it was time.

I slid down before the pony stopped and found our bundle in the tree where I'd hidden it during the night. My hands were shaking as I pulled it toward us, and the clothes, knife, and things fell to the ground.

"You don't have to throw it all in the dirt," Susannah said, kicking her feet out of the stirrups. "You ought to have better sense than that, Beth." She was full of herself, but I scarcely heard her. She was only a little thing.

Right away, she began shucking her girl's clothes. She stood shivering: her skin was pale and goose bumpy, just exactly like a plucked chicken's. "Turn around," she said before slipping out of her shift.

I turned, and tried to untie my kerchief. But my fingers seemed to have frozen. I plucked at the knot without getting anywhere. Behind me, I could hear Susannah shaking out the britches. My hands finally quit moving at all, and I just stared at the trees. I could not move.

"What's wrong with you?" she said, suddenly popping around in front of me. She laughed when she saw how motionless I was. "Can't you even do the simplest little thing? Don't tell me I have to look after you every step of the way, Beth."

I let her untie the knot at my throat and listened to her prattling on. The woods were silent around us. She slipped two buttons of my dress like I was a doll or a child. I began to think I was watching us from up in the pines around us. I saw her in her boy's britches and shirt with her long yellow braids. I saw myself turned to stone, still in my dirt-colored dress and apron. I was turned to stone, but I was starting to shake.

"Beth? Beth?" Susannah peered into my eyes.

"Bethlehem," I croaked.

She was puzzled. "What?"

"My name is Bethlehem."

"It is?" Susannah lifted her shoulders and let them drop. "Why didn't you ever say so before?"

I shook my head and finished unbuttoning my dress. Then I stripped it off and began to put on the other set of boy's clothes.

"It's a real pretty name," she went on. "That's where Jesus Christ was born. Why didn't you tell me?"

That was a harder question than I knew how to answer. Something was in me that wanted to say my real, whole name, and I couldn't stop it if I tried. My skin was as hot as a fire. I had the power to smite boulders into dust, pull trees from the ground, even rise from the earth and fly above it.

Do you hear me, God? I am Bethlehem!

Susannah was looking at me strangely. I just shook my head again and pushed my feet into an old pair of boots. The noises of the forest slowly began to sound in my ears again: the racket of squirrels ransacking through the branches, the calls of birds, the crack of a twig under my heel.

I bowed my head. Now I could begin my life.

SUSANNAH: I decided to take no notice of the strange humor Bethlehem was in. She said her full name out loud a few more times in an experimental tone, but stubbornly refused to answer my questions. I considered it to be fancifulness, and chose not to encourage her in it, so I busied myself with my plan. My first concern was hiding our old clothes. After some thinking, I folded them up small, turned over some large rocks in the stream bed, and buried them there in the water.

"I expect they'll just rot," I said, drying my hands on my britches. I liked the way it felt not to wear skirts, and I jumped from one rock to another just for the novelty of it. Bethlehem stood on the bank.

"You don't even look happy," I said after studying her for a moment. "Here I've gone and brought you along on my escape, and you look as sullen as an old cow. You don't show one bit of gratefulness, either."

Bethlehem found the scissors and unwrapped them. "I'll cut those braids off you if you come on."

I ignored her tone. After all, we should have been hurrying instead of idling along a stream. I climbed up the bank and turned my back to her while she sawed away at my hair. First one braid and then the other fell on the ground next to me like two bits of rope. It gave me a strange pang.

"Do I look like a boy?" I asked, fingering my shorn hair. How strange it was, strange and exciting.

Bethlehem eyed me for a moment. "I expect so."

I eyed her back. Her hair was already short, and without a headcloth, and in britches, she did look enough like a boy to pass. Anyone not looking for girls would readily take us for boys.

I loosened the hair from the braids and let it float off down the stream. "Well, come on if you're coming," I said.

I tied our bundle of gear at my waist, enjoying the rough and roguish effect. Then we climbed back up on the pony and headed north to meet the Shenandoah.

Neither of us spoke for some time. Bethlehem was nursing some secret thoughts of her own, and I was thinking ahead to Vermont. But as the morning warmed, I grew a bit anxious.

"When do you suppose they'll start to miss us?" I asked.

She did not answer.

"Do you suppose they'll send someone out to track us down?"

Bethlehem still did not answer. She trembled slightly.

I was beginning to feel piqued by her silence. It didn't relieve my trepidation at all. "Well, why won't you talk?" I said, twisting around to look at her. "You've hardly said a word since we left the farm."

"I don't guess I've got much to say," she replied.

"Oh, why did I even let you come along?" I continued. "If you ain't going to take the least little bit of enjoyment out of being free, why'd you want to come with me?"

Bethlehem stared at me for a long moment. Then she slid off the pony's back and began walking alongside.

"Now what is it?" I asked her.

"Go on without me," she said, looking at the ground. "We don't noways have to go together."

"But Beth!" She didn't look at me. "Beth!"

She trudged along, gaining a little on the pony, who was only walking.

"Bethlehem!"

At that, she stopped. "What?" she asked me, beginning to sound angry.

I stopped the pony and swung myself down. He took a few steps and began nibbling at some weeds.

"I just don't know what's gotten into you, Bethlehem," I complained. I picked up a small stone and turned it around in my hands. "Just the littlest taste of freedom, and you're acting pretty uppity, it seems like. I thought we were friends."

"Did you?" Bethlehem laughed.

I was abashed. Truthfully, I had never thought it before. Then and there I realized that I had swallowed many a hateful notion about the black race without gagging in the least. And it was only just starting to disagree with me. I felt a bit sick. There was a shifting inside of me, like I was taking a few steps to the side for a different view.

I kicked at some pine needles and fiddled with that stone. I had never much cared for being chastised, especially when it was deserved. You know I'm stubborn.

"Don't you understand the littlest thing?" Bethlehem blazed up. Her eyes looked hot. "I'm running away! Runaway niggers mostly get strung up when they're caught or they feet chopped. Don't you know it?"

"Well, we ain't getting caught!" I retorted. "I don't aim to go back there, either!"

"But if you did, they'd just slap your white hand and say don't you do it again, little Miss Yankee!"

I was indignant. "Oh—" I gasped. I wanted to throw that rock at something. I turned around and let it fly—right into the pony's flank. He let out a squeal and bolted.

Bethlehem and I were both stunned. "Get him!" she yelled.

We both took off running through the trees after him. As I dodged around the trunks, branches slapped in my face and plucked at my clothes, and the awkward bundle of supplies tied at my belt threw off my pace. The pony was far ahead and disappearing fast. I could see Bethlehem through the trees to my right, angling to head him off.

But we were both much too slow for a pony on its way back to its stall. My breath was coming painfully, and I stumbled over roots more than once. At last, I stopped and sank to my knees. Flies settled instantly on my face and neck, nor did I have the heart to shoo them off.

Bethlehem walked back to me without a word and sat down beside me in the leaves and needles.

"It's my fault." I was panting with exertion, and my remorse was growing by the second. "I'm a fool."

"I expect so," Bethlehem said with a heavy sigh. "And I expect that pony will be back to the farm in an hour with that fire under his feet."

She didn't have to say any more. Once the pony returned riderless, the alarm would be sounded. We had to hurry.

"Which way's the stream?" I asked, squinting through the trees.

Bethlehem pointed. "Come on." She led the way.

We retraced our steps through the woods in silence. I felt a heavy burden of guilt and responsibility. My only consolation was that our precious store of supplies was not lost. I had fancied myself a Robin Hood figure. But now I had ample proof of my resourcefulness: I had driven off our only means of transportation.

Sunk in my gloom, I paid scant attention to our course. But Bethlehem stopped suddenly and crouched. I kneeled beside her.

"What is it?" I whispered.

She shook her head, breathing hard through her nose. I watched her in confusion and then listened, and I heard what had alerted her—men's voices, and a clanking sound.

Before I could tell her what to do, Bethlehem was creeping silently forward, keeping low to the ground. I was inclined to be bossy, but Bethlehem never seemed to give me the opportunity. More than wanting to boss, though, I was eager to know who was coming down the trail we had just been on ourselves, so I followed her, not to be outdone in daring and adventurous spirit. We stopped at the growth of vines and bushes that fringed the path.

A grim procession was passing just beyond our screen. Seven black men in chains were filing along the trail, while three white men on horses brought up the rear. By turning my head, I saw that one more white man led the group south.

The slaves moved slowly, with bowed heads and dull eyes. On their backs, I saw welts and dark bruises; and on their wrists and ankles, raw sores from the irons. They were grimed with dirt, blood, and worse, and flies clung to their eyelids undisturbed. The smell of the traders' horses reached my nose, as well as another scent that was harsh and acrid. Nobody spoke. I shivered.

That they were stolen slaves I had no doubt. I had read the same reports of such banditry in the area that Bethlehem says she had seen. It was evident to me that these white men were the same I had read about in the newspaper: traffickers in stolen Negroes.

And at the same instant, I felt sure that our disappearance could be laid at their door. Few citizens cared to tangle with such lawless men, but news of the traffickers' presence in the area would surely be broadcast. Our runaway pony would lend weight to the notion as well.

Once the captives had passed, I turned to Bethlehem to share this observation with her. But her attitude and posture silenced me. Her eyes were closed, and her lips moved in prayer. I waited.

"Bethlehem," I whispered, once she had raised her head.

She opened her eyes and slowly turned on me. "You don't know," she said fiercely. Tears were running down her face. "You can't ever know."

My stomach rolled over. I met her accusation mutely. There was nothing I might say in the face of her grief and outrage. That I had seen the chained slaves only as a convenient story to cover our escape now seemed monstrous to me.

"You're right—I don't know," I admitted. I tried to swallow the bitter taste in my mouth. "I'm sorry. I'm so sorry."

"Your sorry don't help." Bethlehem turned away from me, sobbing bitterly.

I watched her with a grieving heart. Was the pain she felt as deep as mine when my parents died? Or was it deeper or wider, greater in magnitude in some dimension I did not understand? I could not know. But be it only half of what mine had been, I knew that she was in a terrible, dark place.

I moved closer to her and put one arm across her

shoulders. She shook me off, but I was stubborn and hugged her tighter. Then she relented and cried against me, and I cried too. The seriousness of our trek settled around me like a blanket, heavy and dark as night. For the first time, I doubted we would survive, far less succeed. We were in a dark place together, then. We needed everything we had, and God's mercy, to get back into the light again.

1·8·9·6

Free had been silent, staring at her lap. When Gran broke off, Free pushed her chair back and ran into the bedroom. Bethlehem shook her head sadly.

"Why don't you go in and speak to her," she said into the silence.

I looked at Gran, but she was looking at me. I turned a surprised gaze on Bethlehem. "Me?"

"Please. I feel a little tired myself."

"What would I say?" I asked, feeling my face color.

"Say something friendly, child," Gran said in an exasperated tone.

I felt extremely self-conscious, but I rose as I was bidden. Even my steps felt awkward as I crossed the room and tapped on the closed door. When there was no answer, I sent a glance over my shoulder. Gran and Bethlehem were speaking quietly together and did not notice me.

"Oh, shoot," I whispered. I pushed the door open and went into the bedroom.

Free was looking in Bethlehem's small mirror. I had thought she might be crying, or melancholy, to say the least. That she was simply studying her face in the mirror threw me into confusion.

"What do you want?" she asked without turning around.

I hesitated. "I thought you might feel unwell," I offered with a vague gesture.

"What could you do about it?" Free snorted as she stared at me through the mirror.

My face heated again in anger. "I don't know! I could get a cool cloth for your forehead if your head aches, or burn some feathers if you feel faint!"

"I don't feel faint," she said warningly.

"Then I could get you some broth to settle your stomach," I replied, staring back hard.

We confronted each other in silence. Then Free let out one short laugh. I grinned shyly.

"I expect you're always welcome in a sickroom," she said.

I sat on the bed and shook my head. "Well, I'm sorry. I just thought I'd see if you were feeling sad. It's a sad story," I added in a quieter tone.

Free nodded and looked away. "You'll never know how sad." She closed me out again.

But something in me rebelled at that. "I'm sorry I'll never know," I told her. "But does that mean we can't be friendly?"

"I don't know."

I smoothed the coverlet absently with my writing hand. There was an ink stain on one finger. "Shoot," I muttered. I didn't care that it was ungenteel to curse. What did gentility matter? The rain continued to stream monotonously down the windowpanes. I was exhausted.

"Why would you even care to be friendly to me?" Free burst out suddenly.

I looked up at her. "My Gran's friendly with Miss Reid," I observed. "I don't see why we can't be."

"I can see it," Free said, staring at herself in the mirror once more. "I can see it plain as day."

I looked morosely out the window. "I wish this weather would break," I said after a pause. "I do wish it would."

Gran came to the bedroom door then. "It's time to leave," she said. "Bethlehem needs rest."

Free hurried away to her.

Gran came to me and touched my cheek. "You're a good girl, Mary," she said tenderly. I pressed my face against her hand and tried to feel proud. "I'm so glad I brought you."

I couldn't be glad. Not at that time.

"I thought we should—"

Gran stopped herself in midsentence. I looked up to see what had halted her. Frowning, Gran took a few steps toward the wall to study a mounted photograph.

"What is it?" I asked, joining her.

The sepia print showed a small, wood-frame building. It was quite clearly a schoolhouse, with a bell hanging by the door and a scuffed dirt yard. And standing in the open doorway was Bethlehem as a young woman, smiling proudly for the camera and holding three books in her arms. At her side were two older white women, also smiling. Two small black children sat on a log bench nearby.

"Who are they?" I asked, pointing to the white women.

My grandmother compressed her lips for a moment. "Her teachers," she said at last. "Or so I assume."

Her voice sounded oddly bitter to me. I looked at her, wondering. But before I could ask what had upset her, she turned and walked stiffly from the room.

Puzzled, I looked at the photograph again. Bethlehem smiled out at me from the past, safe and free with her Canadian friends.

My head was beginning to ache. I didn't *want* to know why Gran was so distressed. I didn't want to ask.

We made our good-byes and returned to the hotel through the relentless downpour. When the next day dawned wet and dismal again, I wanted to pull the bedclothes over my head. But we went back through the rain to Bethlehem's, and after I read aloud the last few pages of Gran's narrative, Bethlehem took up the story again.

SPRING
1·8·5·5

BETHLEHEM: Seeing the slave coffle made me low, like nothing else, like nothing Byron or Fidelia had ever done to me. Believe it or not, I almost thought I was crazy to run away from Reids' farm, where at least we ate regular and never were beaten. But I was too low to speak at all, and I surely could not move to save my life.

Susannah shook off her tears sooner than I did and had to drag me up by my arm.

"Come on if you're coming," she said. "I wish I didn't chase off that pony, but it's too late now. We'll just have to walk."

I nodded dumbly. I was in her hands.

"Let's share these things out," she went on. "You carry half and I carry half, in case one of us loses everything."

Susannah's spirits lifted higher by the minute, and she fussed like a young mother, separating our gear and handing out decisions.

"Should I carry the lucifer matches? I don't know—I expect I would fall straight into the river if I had them. You carry those, Bethlehem. I'll take the knife. I think that looks better, too, case anybody sees us."

I nodded again. The best way to make white folks nervous was to let them see black folks with knives. I saw myself holding a knife the way a conjure man holds a conjure stick, saw it shiver and tremble and point first toward Byron and then toward Fidelia. It would seek out the secret places. That is the way of these strong things.

"Yes, you best carry that knife," I whispered.

There was no slavery in Vermont, Susannah had said. I prayed she was right. I didn't want to hurt anyone. All her talk was talking me into believing I could stop in Vermont. It sounded sweet and fine.

Once she had it sorted out, who would tote what, she looked as happy as a boy with a frog. She even looked like a boy, too, with her short hair and dirt on her face. I thought, *Who are you?* once as I looked at her. *What are you to me?*

But she was so brisk and brash that she didn't give me time to sink down again. I was whisked along in front of her like a chicken ahead of a broom, a dry leaf in a strong breeze. I was eased by the gratefulness of knowing she could keep me out of that place in my mind where I cut and killed and stamped in blood. If I stuck with Susannah and remembered Jesus, I wouldn't get myself into trouble.

"I'll tell you what I've been thinking," she said. We started walking the trail. "I've been thinking that we'll have to do some stealing for food. I know it ain't right, but I don't see what choice we have. Now that we're on foot, it's going to take a sight longer to get home. God will understand, I know. He's bound to forgive us. He just has to."

I nodded. That sounded like the God I knew, the one who comforted me when I got so low, the one who knew what happened to me and said, *It's all right, child. You'll make it through. Just hold on. Just hold on a while more.*

"I expect He will," I said.

"There!" Susannah turned and smiled at me. "I knew you could talk."

I had to laugh. But it sounded a bit like crying, too. My heart was going in sixteen different directions.

But my body was going North.

"Come on, sonny," Susannah said, swaggering in her britches. "Let's not dawdle like a couple of missish young gals."

"I hear you."

"It's a fine day to run away, ain't it?" Susannah asked. "I like these woods here."

She stood still and tipped her head back.

"This is the forest primeval. The murmuring pines
    and the hemlocks,
Bearded with moss, and in garments green,
    indistinct in the twilight,

Stand like Druids of eld, with voices sad and
    prophetic,
Stand like harpers hoar, with beards that rest
    upon their bosoms.
Loud from its rocky caverns, the deep-voiced
    neighboring ocean
Speaks, and in accents disconsolate answers the
    wail of the forest.

"How do you like that?"

I gawked at her. I didn't know what she was talking about.

"It's part of a poem, silly," Susannah said. "From a book. I know there's no deep-voiced neighboring ocean, but there's a stream, anyway."

She was looking about her at the trees and the moss and such. I didn't know what those Druids were that were standing around, but I didn't want any of them coming after me, especially if it was an evil forest. I wasn't much familiar with poetry in those days.

"Who's dawdling now?" I asked her.

Susannah hitched up her britches. "That's me, I guess. Let's go."

SUSANNAH: Our first day of traveling was strange and wonderful. Our hopes could not help but dash headlong before us up the trail. Yet we were startled by each unusual sound. We expected to hear the shouts and shots of hot pursuit at every turning.

I didn't speak of my main worry to Bethlehem. I had read of Abolition men from New York or Boston being tried and jailed for stealing slaves in order to free them. I just knew something dreadful would befall me if we were caught, but whether I feared the law or my uncle more, I did not know.

For the main, we walked without speaking much. Both of us were absorbed in our private thoughts. From time to time, when I thought of the trouble I might catch, I felt myself grow angry and resentful toward Bethlehem. She had profoundly altered my plans and responsibilities by coming along.

But when I looked at her, walking with her dark face raised to catch a sight or a sound of the forest and her eyes filled with something I could not see, then I softened toward her. It would have been a fearful journey to undertake alone. But I was not alone.

This knowledge lifted my heart. In an instant, I was alive to the beauty of the surrounding woods, to the quality of light that slanted down onto the path and illuminated our way; I trembled with wonder at the sharp and resinous smell of pines and the touch of the moist air on my skin. Beside us, the constant noisy business of the stream kept step with us, now straying away on some errand of its own, now muttering and purling along at our feet. Jays flashed out of the shadow and vanished again, and the delicate commotion of startled deer pattered into the distance. I was enjoying myself capitally. I remember it was hot.

All this time, because our pace was slower on foot than on horseback, and because the threat of pursuit made us anxious to put distance behind us, we had not stopped except for the shortest of rests. By dusk, I was tired and very hungry.

Bethlehem was walking as tall as ever.

"It'll be dark soon," I said as I stepped onto a fallen tree. The bark was loose and damp and gave off a mossy odor when crushed under my boots.

"Yes," Bethlehem agreed.

I jumped down and glanced sidelong at her. She didn't seem to be hungry or tired, either one. I was piqued. You know by now Bethlehem has as forceful a will as I do; she may laugh at me for this. But because that childish bossiness was so strong in me, and I saw myself as our natural leader, it just didn't seem right that I would be the weaker of us: I tried to ignore the hollowness in my stomach. We walked on while the light faded. I wanted her to ask for a halt.

"Well, we'll have to stop and make a camp somewhere," I added, keeping my tone practical and authoritative and praying my stomach wouldn't growl. "We don't want to risk getting lost in the dark."

"That's right."

I stared at her back as she gained a few paces on me. Much to my chagrin, tears sprang to my eyes.

"Well, can't we stop now?" I wailed.

Bethlehem turned. Her face was shadowed, but I saw a tired smile.

"I'm ready," she said, at once sitting down on the ground.

"What, here?" I looked back over my shoulder. We were still in the trail. "That don't make the least bit of sense."

She nodded and caught her breath in a long sigh. When I realized she was as tired as I was, but just as stubborn and proud about letting it show, I broke a switch and swatted a tree trunk with it, giving her some time.

She was first-rate. That's what I was thinking.

"Say, Bethlehem?" I picked at the bark on a tree. "If I sometimes call you Beth, does that sit all right with you? Only seeing as how Bethlehem is such an uncommon long name."

She thought it over. "I suppose that would do all right. Sometimes."

First-rate, I thought again. I was glad.

When we were both rested enough to continue, we struck away from the path, into the woods. I was all for building a fire, but Bethlehem argued persuasively against it. We made a cold camp, eating a little of the biscuit and praying to get out of Virginia as fast as we could.

We fell asleep with our heads pillowed upon our folded arms, and I dreamed of Vermont. What Bethlehem dreamed of I don't know.

1·8·9·6

"What do you think I dreamed of?" Bethlehem asked us.

I didn't know. How could I have guessed? I looked down at the paper in front of me for the answer.

"Freedom," Free replied with a rapt expression. "Freedom."

"Oh." I bit my lip on the exclamation and shook my head. "Of course."

Bethlehem gave us all a smile of profound gladness. "Dreaming doesn't get any better than that, girls."

We were all glad with her. Somehow, imperceptibly, the mood in the small room had lightened. To our great relief, the rain had finally let up. Outside, the sky was lifting rapidly, and our spirits along with it. Noah and his family could not have been more grateful for the end of the Deluge.

My grandmother had laughed at herself when Bethlehem recited from "Evangeline," and Bethlehem had chuckled over their battle of wills in the woods. "I wasn't about to be weaker than a skinny white girl," Bethlehem said to Gran. "But I sure was glad when you said quit!"

I smiled across the table at Free. She met my gaze and smiled in return. She had a dimple. When I glanced at Gran, she was watching us both with a thoughtful, contented expression.

"Then what happened, Mrs. Emmons?" Free asked.

"Then what happened?" Gran echoed. "Then everything happened."

"We joined the Great Valley Road," Bethlehem explained. "We did pass for boys, and nobody noticed us much. If anyone asked, Susannah always said we were going up to Winchester, or Frederick, or whatever the nearest town was, to visit cousins by the name of Cheatham."

My grandmother smiled gleefully at Bethlehem. "I'll tell you what else happened," she said, turning back to us girls with an air of conspiracy. "Bethlehem decided she preferred being—"

"Don't you go telling tales, now," Bethlehem broke in. She stood up and fussed with the pages on which Free and I had taken turns with the dictation. Then she crossed to the window and rubbed at an invisible smudge on the pane. "That was just some foolishness of mine. It doesn't come into account."

Free and I were wide-eyed.

"Just pretend I never told you," Gran continued,

lowering her voice and leaning toward us. She cast her old friend an impish look. We could tell Bethlehem was listening closely and trying to look severe and schoolmistressish.

"She told me more than once that she preferred being a boy and planned to keep up the masquerade for the rest of her life. She observed that nobody bothers boys—boys can do whatever they want and go anywhere. We saw some things we never would have been allowed to watch in skirts."

My color rose. I burned to know what *things* they had seen, but it would be unseemly to ask. One look at Free told me she was aching to ask as well. But neither of us could.

"You wanted to stay a boy?" Free ventured at last.

Bethlehem turned around with a self-deprecating laugh. "Well, I never had known such license. When I wore britches, no man touched me or stared at me or said things to make me ashamed. I didn't have to walk small."

I shifted on my chair and crossed my ankles. The heavy fabric of my dress hung across my legs like a blanket, and I twitched it aside.

Boys, I thought, don't need half an hour to dress.

Just thinking of wearing britches made my pulse beat faster—in mortification or in excitement? I didn't know. A parade of images from books and magazines suddenly crowded my memory: Nebraska girls galloping their paint ponies like wild Indians, Mrs. Amelia Bloomer demonstrating the "rational dress" costume for ladies, the Chinese women in New York in wide-legged pants and quilted jackets, Rosa Bonheur in men's clothes painting horses at the Paris slaughterhouse, actress Fanny Kemble in a vest and britches. My friend Amy and I had laughed over them all so smugly in our Gramercy Park homes.

Now those women did not seem so comic, so despicable.

"I enjoyed being a boy, too," Gran said.

"And didn't the ladies love those big blue eyes of yours, too," Bethlehem cackled. " 'Here, son, have this nice piece of cherry pie.' "

It was Gran's turn to blush. "I never asked for it."

"You should have seen her." Bethlehem was warming to her tale. "Just the sweetest little white boy you ever saw. Ladies nearly fell over themselves trying to put a little weight on him. He seemed to be so delicatelike."

"Now, that's quite enough of that," Gran blustered.

We were laughing. "What else?" Free asked. "What else did they say?"

" 'Who's your mother, son?' " Bethlehem mimicked. " 'Have another cup of cider. Have some more biscuits and gravy. I declare, you have hair like an angel's.' "

Gran was the only one of us not howling. She

straightened her back very primly. "It all went into curls when I cut it short," she explained, only adding to our hilarity.

"And nobody knew?" I asked. I tried to catch my breath.

"We thought we were home and clear," Gran said. "We were gone two weeks without a bit of worry. We crossed the Potomac on a boatload of horses bound for Baltimore and took turns spitting into the current, as boys will. Sometimes we rode for miles on a farmer's wagon, and we were making steady progress. The weather was fair, the way was mountainous but clear, and people were generous. There wasn't a cloud in the sky, as they say."

Bethlehem glanced out the window. "I doubt there's a cloud in the sky right now, either. You girls go on out and get some air. You have been cooped up too long. Go on and take a walk, and while you're out, pick up some sausages and bread."

We were suddenly shy. I glanced at Free. "I could enjoy a walk," I mumbled.

"But I should stay—" she began.

"Go on, Free," Bethlehem insisted. "I don't need you every blessed moment of the day."

Free stood up with obvious reluctance. "Are you sure?"

Instead of answering, Bethlehem took us both by the arm and marched us to the door. We giggled as she shooed us out onto the landing.

"Come on," Free said.

Together we walked out onto the street, from which Free led us to one of the avenues a few blocks away. There was naturally some constraint between us, considering the strangeness of our being out walking together. We strolled without speaking, stopping occasionally to peer in a shop window. Sunlight cast a wash of brilliance across the still-wet streets. I felt newly made, full of potentialities.

I was highly conscious of our silence and searched for something to say. Conversing with my school friends had always been easy and was always helped along by a generous give-and-take of compliments.

As we walked, I was struck by a thought: if I wanted to compliment Free, I would have said that she had an elegant neck and very nice ears. A noble head well set upon an elegant neck was the hallmark of beauty that I had learned from my friends. Somewhat to my surprise, Free fit the description to a tee.

While this realization gained a surer foothold in me, I became quite proud of myself. I was judicious, temperate, and fair. I could see the good and the beauty in everything, and I felt full of the whole world. I might become a missionary, I thought. I might go to Africa or China or Polynesia. I would be known by a quaint native epithet. People would look up to me.

At that moment, walking down High Street with Free, I was filled with the love of God and all His creation. I was exalted. All this, because I thought Free was pretty.

I considered mentioning the discovery of Free's beauty to Amy, but she would be scandalized at such a suggestion, I was sure, and would mock me for finding beauty in a black girl. I stole a look at Free. I could tell Gran, I knew, and she would not be scandalized. I resolved to tell Gran that evening at our hotel.

But then, the swift passage of a horse and carriage arrested my attention. Through the open window, I caught a glimpse of a classical profile, blonde curls, and a dainty hat. The vision was gone in a rush and clatter of wheels. I stopped in my tracks.

"Is something wrong?" Free asked, also stopping.

I blushed. "Oh, it's nothing."

We both looked ahead, aware of a commotion some yards up the sidewalk. People were streaming around some obstruction, eddying past and bustling on. Free craned her neck to see and continued walking.

"Someone must have fallen down," I observed, but Free had already hurried ahead.

I appealed to a woman coming toward me. "Is it an accident?"

"Only an old colored man," the woman replied.

I saw Free kneel by a slumped figure. I started and stopped uncertainly. It seemed that all of cosmopolitan Toronto was walking past me, men and women smartly turned out, girls my own age. In some confusion, I met the eyes of a girl in a velvet-trimmed walking coat. She returned my stare blankly.

"Free," I called, going a few hesitant steps nearer. My throat closed up.

The old man was bald except for a thin ring of white hair around his pate, and the papery skin beneath his eyes drooped wearily. His coat was shiny with age; his trousers showed a carefully mended tear on one knee. He sat, with Free's assistance, and shook his head.

"It came over me, just suddenly," he said in a wondering voice. "Just a darkness all around me."

"Let me help you," Free said loudly. "Can you stand up, sir?"

"Just a darkness," he repeated in the same dazed manner.

My face burned. I could hardly walk away from Free, but that was what I most wanted to do. Then I saw blood on his palm where he had cut himself on the bricks. I leaned closer, my heart pounding.

"I don't have a handkerchief," Free said, patting her pockets. "Can I have yours?"

"Mine?" I gaped at her.

She raised her eyes to my face and regarded me reproachfully. I stared back, knowing suddenly that I had failed. Without another word, I reached into my pocket and pressed my lace-trimmed handkerchief to his hand.

"There," I said breathlessly. "You'll be all right."

While Free helped him to stand, I stood staring, dumbfounded, at the pavement. It seemed to me that there were deep chasms gaping on all sides, opening and closing without warning. I hadn't seen the one that yawned open at my feet until I fell into it. I had just been walking along, and before I knew it, I'd stumbled and fallen in. I was even more stupefied than the old man.

Give me a map, I wanted to say, a map that shows where in the path those deep chasms are.

I wanted to go back to that part of the street where I could have told Free I thought she was pretty, where I should have told her I could think so.

Instead, she and I performed our errands in painful silence and retraced our steps to Bethlehem's. We didn't comment to Gran and Bethlehem about our walk, and I resumed my place at the table with a heavy heart. My hands ached from writing, but I took up the task again, bewildered and penitent.

SUMMER
1·8·5·5

BETHLEHEM: It's time to move ahead now to Emmitsburg, Maryland. We had earned our way some days by chopping kindling or such other middling chores at the middling-sized farms scattered here and there. Mostly our pay was supper and a place to sleep, but one kindly woman on the road to Emmitsburg gave Susannah a few pennies for the job I did cleaning out a smokehouse. No doubt it was that pretty hair again.

So when we reached town, Susannah had it in her mind to get us some candy. I told her I didn't need it, since I had never tasted any and wasn't of a mind to try it. But licorice stick was what she wanted, and she would have some. I waited for her outside the store and kept myself to myself.

Folks passed by me. I think that store was the post office, too. Nobody paid me any mind, but I was as jumpy as a cat in a kennel. Being in a town with many people always made me that way. On the road or in the woods, passing as a boy only meant fooling a handful of people in a day. In town, our chances of being discovered were that much bigger.

I scuffed my feet in the dust. Susannah was taking too long a time choosing the candy. I knew she liked the risk of acting the boy in front of folks, but I was on fire to get going. Every minute strung me out tighter and more tense.

I heard a heavy footfall behind me on the boards, and then a body lurched into me. I went sprawling and scrambled to my feet.

"Goddamn you, boy," a thick voice said.

He was a cracker, a dirt-poor farmer in for seed corn or nails or such supplies. His red, pitted face showed him to be a dedicated drinker, and his cheek bulged with chaw. His beard was stained with it. One of his eyes wandered, but he hit me with a hard stare anyway, spit, and scratched himself.

"Whose nigger air you?" he demanded.

I rubbed my sweating hands on my britches and kept looking down. "I belongs to Sam Cheatham, mass. He in the store."

A long, mean silence sizzled between us. He was half-drunk and itching to abuse someone. Every cord and sinew in my body was ready to run, but I stayed still and silent. If he hit me, I would have to hit him back. That was what a few days of freedom had done to me, and it would land me in leg irons or a collar or worse.

"You—" He went on muttering drunkenly, disgustingly, and sniffing hard. He brought out every vile and revolting curse in the calendar and flung them at my head like handfuls of filth.

"Thas sho right, mass," I said, nodding and grinning.

He stared at me blearily for another long moment. I tasted gall in my throat. I hated him even more than he hated me and my kind. He was everything bad summed up in one cruel, ignorant self, everything I was running from: a pocked and stinking Goliath. But I knew myself as a David. If I had had a gun, I would have used it as easily on him as on a copperhead.

Jesus, Jesus. Don't let me kill this man!

Beyond, something caught his attention. With a hoglike grunt, he pushed by me and staggered away. I knew his mules or his brats would feel his fist soon.

"Susannah," I prayed, my eyes shut tight. "Hurry."

I hovered at the entrance to the store. I could hear her voice, her laugh, from inside. She was charming someone. Dropping her girl's clothes had made her drop her shyness and become bold, and people found her a fine, fresh-faced, sassy boy. I thought I would scream if she stayed another minute longer. My shirt stuck to my wet back.

A woman approached the door from behind me, so I quickly stepped aside. That was when I saw the notice. I puzzled it out, my hands shaking all the while at my sides.

RUN AWAY
from the farm of
Reverend Reid of Front Royal:

Two girls, aged thirteen.
His niece, SUSANNAH MCKNIGHT
with blonde hair, fair complected.
His slave, BETH, very dark-skinned
Negress with good teeth.

Believed to be traveling North.

The sound of wind filled my ears.

"What are you staring at, son?"

Dazed, I turned and found myself face-to-face with a black woman in a red scarf. She reminded me so much of Lizer that I nearly grabbed her hand in my panic.

Help me! I screamed inside.

"Son?" she said again.

There was doubt in her voice, and her eyes went wary. Her glance touched upon my chest and flicked up again. "What are you playing at?" she whispered.

People were walking past us, their boots loud and hollow on the wooden steps. A breeze fanned across me, chilling the sweat on my forehead. A bee shot by my cheek.

"Ma'am—" I couldn't speak. Fear and lonesomeness were choking me.

"Ben? Step along, now."

Susannah had come out of the shop, sucking on a licorice stick. There was a paper twist in her other hand. She jerked her head for me to follow and gave the woman a friendly smile.

"Excuse us," she said with elaborate, mock courtesy. "Me and Ben is in an awful hurry."

The woman gave Susannah a level stare and turned back to me. Nobody spoke. A dog barked away down the dusty street while we faced off. I saw Susannah's color rise and her mouth drop open. She looked suddenly small and childish with the black sugar on her tongue.

"Git," the woman said, tucking in the corners of her lips. "I never saw you. Jes' git."

We didn't speak. We turned and hurried away. I could only think of getting out of town before I did something bad. We broke into a run and made for the back of a stable, where we crouched beside a wall hot with sun. Wasps, drunk from the heat, smacked lazily against the tin-colored boards.

"My lord, she knew," Susannah said. Her eyes were huge.

I was breathing hard. "No more towns. I can't take no more towns."

She nodded and gulped for air.

"No more going on the roads, neither," I said.

She nodded again. Then she stared down at her hand. She still clutched her licorice stick, and her fingers were black with it. A wasp hovered. With a shudder, Susannah flung the candy away from her into the grass.

"I won't let them get you, Bethlehem," she breathed. She looked up and met my eyes. "I swear by God I won't."

I know she meant it. But there was something bigger and stronger than her that wouldn't let it be true.

———

SUSANNAH: It frightened me thoroughly to have such a close call in Maryland. Sentiments in that state were sharply divided on the question of slavery, and somehow I had gotten it into my head that we would be fine. I had expected to encounter difficulties in Virginia, where in fact we went unaccosted. Bethlehem relayed to me the news of my uncle's advertisement. It chilled me.

My understanding of the Fugitive Slave Act was hazy at best. I knew runaways could be apprehended anywhere, and had even seen it happen in Bennington. But still, I had hoped that the feelings of people would be more favorably disposed toward us the further north we went. I had hoped we would have less and less to fear.

I hadn't the heart to tell Bethlehem my chiefest concern, though perhaps she already knew the truth herself: until I got her to Vermont, we were not safe. This, at least, is what I thought. I honestly believed all would be well when we reached my home; in my mind it was a haven from all evils.

When we were recovered from our scare and had gathered our belongings from their hiding place in an empty skunk hole, we commenced our journey again.

"What I propose to do is follow the road but not walk on it," I said as we shouldered our burdens.

Bethlehem shook her head. "No people," she insisted.

"Ain't that what I'm telling you? We'll keep a couple stone's throws off from it, in the woods. And no more stopping at houses to do jobs or get food."

I would miss the pies and the biscuits. "But we don't want to get lost," I added. "We might just end up back in Virginia."

She gave me a hard look, and I kicked a rock.

"And you can stick hidden whenever we get near people," I went on. "If we need anything, I'll go get it by myself. I won't even knock on doors anymore. I'll steal."

Bethlehem nodded silently. She watched her feet walking. I suspected some powerful force lay behind that trembling wordlessness. It made me itch.

While we tramped along, I tried to imagine myself without her. I shut my eyes to Bethlehem, blocked my ears to the sound of her steps. I pictured her clear away from me. For the moment, I was entirely alone:

coldness and darkness flooded in with a fearsome roar and flung me into a void.

Then I heard our matched footsteps again and breathed easier. Her footsteps would always sound alongside mine, I believed. She would always be there, and that certainty filled me with peacefulness.

I opened my eyes and looked at her.

"Well, what do you think of that plan?" I asked.

"I don't want to see nobody."

"You don't have to!" I nearly stamped my foot. But I remembered that look on her face outside the store. And I had vowed to protect her.

I looked down and saw her hand swinging at her side. Her fingers were curled into a tight fist.

"You won't have to," I promised, reaching for her hand.

At first, I thought she would pull it away from me. Then her fingers twined with mine, and we walked hand in hand for several paces without speaking.

"That's fine, then," Bethlehem breathed. She gently released her hand, and pointed off to the right, into the trees and brush. "Let's go. We'll walk with the foxes from here on."

BETHLEHEM: That was in the free state of Maryland. What was Susannah thinking of, still believing I could go with her to Vermont? There was no

such animal as a free state, not for a black soul, and
even as ignorant as I was, I knew it by then. I had
hoped, for a time, that Vermont could be home to me,
but where is home for a runaway slave? Where's home
for the ones who are kidnapped before they even are
born? I saw it was a longer road ahead than I had ever
guessed, and I am on it, still.

Susannah didn't see that, though. She hiked along
by my side, chattering away about her Bennington,
her Battenkill River, her Vermont. She told me I
would love it there. She told me we would go to
school side by side, eating maple sugar candy. There
was a fine picture in her eyes that made her blind to
the true sights before her.

I could have told her that just wanting something
won't make it so. I'd been wanting all my life with no
answer and no relief.

But I said nothing. That day was still to be lived
out, and the next and the next. It was all I could do to
keep putting one foot ahead of the other without fear
that I might step down into the jaws of a trap. Every
gust of hot air on my neck was the foul breath of that
poisonous man outside the store. Everything was a
danger to me. Every noise clutched my heart like a
fist.

A shotgun went off somewhere far away. The
sound cracked woodenly through the heavy air and
echoed in my head. Neither of us moved or spoke.
The fading sound hung between us like a spirit.

Israelites ran from Egypt. Pharaoh chased them.

"I expect that's just someone hunting squirrels," Susannah said, rubbing her hands on her britches. "Don't you expect that's what that is?"

The voice was Fidelia's. I pushed her aside and started to run.

SUSANNAH: I fell over backwards, she shoved me so hard. Stunned, I watched her hurdle over logs and dodge trees. She was getting away from me fast.

"Bethlehem!" I screamed. I scrambled up as fast as I could and chased after her. "Stop!"

She never even looked back, but kept running. Water sprayed up as she crossed a stream, and a moment later I was splashing through it myself, turning my ankles on the rocks.

"Stop!" I yelled again, terrified and surprised both.

The ground now was damp in many places, and a moldering, wet odor fumed up at my every footstep. I didn't know why Bethlehem was running from me, and I was crying from the sudden, dreadful mystery of it. The footing was treacherous. Once, the ground sucked at my boot and nearly wrenched it off. I lunged away with a cry.

Ahead of me, Bethlehem was in the same fix. She bogged up to one knee in peat and began struggling wildly.

"Bethlehem!"

I was closing the distance between us. Just as I reached her, she freed herself but then dropped to her hands and knees, her eyes closed. She breathed in harsh, rasping sobs of air.

"It's me, it's me," I cried, staring down at her in grief and dismay. "Why'd you run away from me? Why?"

She hung her head. Tears coursed her face.

"Bethlehem, why did you run from me?"

At last, she drew herself up and attempted to stand. I knew I should reach out to help her, but I was too dazed. That she would run from me and leave me all alone was an enormity.

"We're going to Vermont together," I said in a bewildered voice. "I don't understand you."

"No."

"No?" I gaped at her stupidly. "What—"

"I am not going to Vermont," she said, and walked some steps away across the thick mat of the bog.

As she moved, the ground swelled under my feet, rolling with sickening flexuousness. I grabbed a tree trunk.

"Not going to Vermont?" I said. I could not comprehend her words.

"I'm going to Canada. It's a real place, ain't it? With people and houses and all?"

I could not get my balance. Slender trees around us swayed lithely, although there was no breeze. My stomach rose and fell with the liquid motion under-foot. I thought I would retch.

"Sure, it's a real place, but I'm going to Vermont." My mind hung on to that one steady thing. Canada? *Canada*? I had had no idea that this was in her mind. I could not credit it at all. "You're going with me. Why, I *stole* you, Bethlehem."

She turned with violent speed, setting the ground moving again. Her breath came fast, but her words came out slow and quiet. "I stole my *self*."

"Yes, you did, you did," I agreed eagerly, desperate to appease her. "But you have to come home with me. It's what we agreed. We *must* stay together! Canada's just miles and miles from home!"

Bethlehem dug the heels of her hands into her eyes, drawing a deep breath and letting it out. She brought her hands away and looked at me bleakly.

"You could go with me."

"I—" My throat closed up and choked my words. Bethlehem. Home. How could I not have both?

We stared at each other, we two, while the elemental, slow undulations of the bog ebbed and flowed beneath us. There were no sounds but our own uncertain breaths. We neither of us could name this new thing between us.

"Let's get out of this place," Bethlehem said, turning away with the question unspoken and un-answered.

The ground heaved again, throwing me to my knees, where I dropped my head and was sick.

Five nights later, while Bethlehem stayed hidden, I sneaked toward a light in the woods. It was a typical dirt farm, scratched out in a clearing among oaks and pines. I waited for a while to see if there might be dogs, but if there were any, they were off hunting up *their* dinner. A mosquito danced in front of my face. I blew at it, and it whined away.

When I felt sure all was quiet, I eased along the tree line toward a shed that looked promising. Even before I heard the chickens, I smelled them. I stopped a minute and clasped my hands.

"Forgive me, Lord. You know the particulars of our case at the present moment, being hungry and all."

God might blink at my undertaking. I prayed he might.

With one eye on the light at the low-ridged house, I unlatched the chickens' trap door and then crawled in on my elbows. Dust and bits of straw went up my nose so that I had to struggle not to sneeze. The effort fairly made my ears pop. In the dark, the hens were making their foolish clucks: *buck-buck-what? buck-what?* I gentled them as best I could and groped for eggs. There were only four. I tied them up in the tail of my shirt, where they felt warm and round and solid to my hand.

"Good-night, ladies. Thank you," I whispered, backing out again.

Elated with my success, I tiptoed out of the clearing and slipped back into the woods. The darkness was profound. I knew a moment of dread. What if I could not find my way back to where Bethlehem waited for me? What if she thought I had abandoned her? What if I was heading clear away from her in the totally wrong direction? What if she were gone? What if I never saw her again?

These anxious thoughts jabbered at me as I stumbled blindly among the trees. Then I tripped over a root and fell.

"The eggs!" I yelped.

"Shh!" Bethlehem's whisper was right by my ear.

"I found you!" I said, with relief. The eggs were intact.

"I found *you*. You sounded like a bunch of hogs coming through those trees."

"Never mind that." I was so glad she was there. My greatest fear was that she would vanish utterly, and finding her in the dark was a nearly paralyzing relief. "I got us four eggs. But I don't know how we'll get them cooked."

We were walking quietly deeper into the woods to the glade we had found before nightfall. A little star-light filtered down, at least enough to see each other dimly against a deeper blackness.

Bethlehem waited while I fumbled the eggs out of

their nest in my shirt. I handed her two. "We'll just eat them raw," she said matter-of-factly. "I've done it plenty."

"Raw?" My voice squeaked.

"I didn't bring no griddle" was her reply.

I nodded meekly. In the darkness I could barely see the white egg as Bethlehem raised it to her mouth. She cracked it against her teeth and tossed the shell aside.

"Just swallow it?" I turned my eggs over in my palm. They were luminous as moons. "What if this one's old? What if it's a hatcher?"

"If you don't want it . . ." she warned. I heard the faint crackle as she broke her second egg against her teeth.

I squared my shoulders. "Oh, I'll do it." I squeezed my eyes shut, lifted the egg, smacked it sharply against my teeth and let the insides slip down my throat. I gagged once when it was down.

"Lord," I whispered, swallowing hard. "I didn't like that."

"I'd eat dirt if I had to." Bethlehem hunkered down against a tree. She sounded tired.

But I was restless. Worrying about Bethlehem and stealing the eggs, as well as the disgust I felt at eating them, had excited my senses into a state of nervous agitation. I stood up and swung my arms about.

"I wish I had taken a chicken instead," I muttered. "I could enjoy a roasted chicken right now."

Bethlehem didn't answer.

"And a piece of pound cake," I went on, dreamily. "My mother bought raisins one time and baked them in a pound cake. That was the best thing I ever ate. What was the best thing you ever ate, Beth?"

She stirred. "I tasted ham once. That was *some* good."

"I like it, too." Still restless, I flung myself down on the ground and rummaged about in my bundle of things.

"Quit jumping around," Bethlehem said in a tired voice.

"I am." I was trying to feel for my last bit of biscuit, when a hot pain sheared up my arm and I cried out.

"What?" Bethlehem sat upright.

I squeezed my fingers together in the agony of pain and shock. "I cut myself on the knife," I gasped.

"Bad?"

I gulped hard. "I think—I don't know."

"Suck on it," she ordered, crouching at my side.

When I put my fingers to my mouth, I felt them slippery. My hand was throbbing already. I thought I would vomit from the metal taste of blood.

There was a ripping sound in the dark, and Bethlehem pulled my hand away from my mouth. She wrapped it tightly in some cloth and pressed her fingers around mine.

"We'll take a good look when it's light," she whispered.

"Yes." I was trying hard not to cry, but not having much luck with it. Tears just welled up and slid down my face no matter how much I wanted them to stop. "Don't leave me."

Bethlehem kept her hand tight around mine and put her other arm across my shoulders. "You picked a bad time to hurt yourself," she said gently. "But you'll be fine, Susannah. You'll be fine."

It was the first time I could remember her saying my name. I nodded, too pained to say anything more. When I looked up, I beheld a patch of the heavens framed by trees. Across that spangled blackness trailed two shooting stars, burning themselves out in the icy firmament. For the moment, that brief meteor splendor banished all thought of weariness and orphanhood from my head. Then the pain returned, and I had to close my eyes against it.

Neither of us slept that night, but we didn't talk much. I still don't know where we were.

1·8·9·6

Gran stopped speaking. She clasped her hands together tightly and looked down at them. Her face was pale.

"Sue—" Bethlehem began.

"I believe we should be going," Gran interrupted. "It's late. I know Mary must be tired."

I smiled to reassure her. "No, I'm not, Gran."

She did not return my smile. "I have a responsibility to you, Mary. I brought you here and I have to look after you."

"But, Gran—"

"No buts," she said sharply, rising from her seat. "It's time I took you back to the hotel."

I looked from Free to Bethlehem in pained surprise. I was embarrassed to be used as the cause of this interruption. I was embarrassed for my grandmother, too.

"We'll be back first thing," she said without looking at Bethlehem.

Against my further objections, Gran was implacable. In short order, we were out in the street, hailing a cab. The strange intensity of Gran's mood made me silent. She looked quite grim. We sat in the cab, each of us looking out our respective windows. I didn't dare speak.

"You haven't said a word about your walk with Free this morning," Gran spoke up abruptly.

Her reminder brought all the shame and disappointment creeping back again. I shook my head. "No."

"Well? Did Free say something unkind to you? You looked so downcast when you returned," Gran said, eyeing me with a forbidding expression.

I stared at her. "No," I said, baffled. "Free never said a word against me. We just walked."

"Where did you go?" In a moment, Gran rounded on me and took my arm in a tight grip. "Did you go somewhere you shouldn't have? Is that why you won't tell me the truth?"

Something akin to horror stole upon me as I looked at Gran's angry face. "No," I whispered. She was hurting my arm.

"Don't lie to me, Mary. I won't have you lying to me." Her hand was beginning to shake, and there were tears in her eyes.

My heart sank within me. "Gran, we only took a short walk, bought the food, and came back," I said, trying not to cry. "Only a few blocks."

She stared at me fiercely for another long moment, and then, releasing my arm, she sank back against the seat. "I'm sorry, Mary," she said, closing her eyes. "I'm overwrought. Please forgive me."

"Of course," I replied, taking her hand and kissing it.

I pressed her hand against my cheek. I felt obscurely wounded. Gran's outburst had broken something inside me. I had never seen in her such volatility, such anger, such unhappiness before. It made me fear for her.

"Gran, dear, perhaps we should go home," I said, tucking her hand through my arm. "Don't you want to go home?"

Gran opened her eyes and stared forlornly through the window. "I've been trying to go home ever since my parents died, Mary."

My heart twisted again. I ached for her. "Oh, Gran."

I rested my cheek against her shoulder. She sounded so lonesome, and there was nothing I could do for her.

"I've made so many, many mistakes." She sighed. "I'm not going to make another. We'll stay to the end."

I nodded. I wanted to stay to the end as well.

When we returned to our hotel, Gran shook off her sorrow and was nearly her old self again. Yet I continued to hear echoes of her passionate voice in my ear. She would never be quite her old self to me.

Yet I think I loved her more.

In the morning, I was solicitous to her every need. She had become fragile in my eyes. I looked anxiously for signs of that pain when we went back to Bethlehem's rooms, but she greeted her old friend with as warm a smile as ever.

"Where did we leave off?" Gran asked, looking over Free's shoulder at the pages of dictation.

"You had hurt yourself," Free said.

Gran shook her head. "What a fool I am," she said quietly. "What a fool."

SUMMER
1·8·5·5

BETHLEHEM: A bird woke me up. It sat just
above us in the tree and carried on like Judgment
Day. My stomach felt to be the size of an acorn.

"Don't let me catch you," I told the rabbling bird.
"Or I'll eat you."

"I hope you ain't talking to me," Susannah murmured. Her knees were stained brown with
blood.

I touched her hand. "How is it?"

"How do you think? It hurts plenty."

The light grew as we began to examine her wound.
The bandage was stiff and stuck in places to her hand
with black scabs of dried blood and dirt. Susannah
was white around the lips by the time I had it off.
Fresh blood welled out from the cut, which started on
the inside of her middle finger and bit deep across her
palm. I saw her pale fingers shake.

"What did you use, a hatchet?" I whispered.

She looked at me and wanted to smile. I could see

she wanted to smile. But that wasn't what her mouth did.

"I would have tried a hatchet myself," I went on, "if I wanted to take my hand off. Let me just put this cloth back on. That'll heal up fine."

"I expect so," Susannah said. She sniffed, and swiped her nose against her shoulder. "It hardly even hurts now."

I didn't say anything. I looked around for something that might be good on that cut, some moss or some likely looking mud. But I didn't know what to use. I never had paid much mind to healing and dosing. I knew clabber was cool on a burn, and tobacco and spit would soothe a wasp sting. But I didn't know what was good on a bad cut.

And listen, a real bad cut was what Susannah had.

"Let me tote your bundle," I said.

Susannah hitched it clumsily under her left arm. "You don't have to do that."

I knew she had that same bad and itchy feeling she had when she first came to the farm, not wanting to be beholden to a slave. But I wasn't a slave, not anymore.

"I know I don't have to. I'm doing it just the same."

I slipped the bundle away from her and started walking. I thought she might want to stop in that glade awhile, but I had it in mind to get moving as soon as we could. What with Susannah being hurt, there was no telling what would happen next. Best to be always going ahead, I thought.

If we stopped, we might not start again.

Also, I didn't like the look of the weather. It was light, but a gray, dismal kind of light. It felt like rain.

"I could use another couple or three eggs," Susannah said, trudging along.

I smiled. "Raw?"

"Shells, too."

"Someday, I aim to eat anything I want, whenever I want it," I told her. "Someday, I aim to be fat."

She grinned. "Back in Bennington, I once saw a man so fat he got stuck in a door. Took my pa and another man to push him back out."

"Is that right?"

"Honest," she said.

Susannah's brow was creased. I noticed her look down at her hand often. I knew it was giving her considerable pain, but she wasn't saying a word of it.

It began to rain.

"I guess we'll get wet," Susannah said. Her voice was small. She wearily lifted her good hand to push aside a branch.

I nodded. My mind was uneasy. But there was nothing to do but keep going. At first, the trees kept us fairly dry. But the downpour turned hard and steady, and in no time we were wet through. Water trickled down the back of my neck and seeped into the cracks in my shoes. My stomach creaked like an old saddle.

"Let's walk faster," I said. "We'll be warmer."

Susannah just nodded. She had tucked her bandaged hand under her arm to keep it dry, but this pose made for an awkward gait. The yellow curls that had pleased the ladies so were stuck to her forehead. Water dripped from her lashes and her nose. She might have been crying, but I didn't like to ask. It would have shamed her.

We went on this way for some time. There was no sign of clearing skies, and I was sure we'd be sleeping wet that night. Wet and hungry. It made me tired just thinking about it.

"I'll tell you what," I said, stepping around a rock. The rain created a mist all about us and hissed down the trees, but it was no help with the mosquitoes. "I believe that reading you taught me is getting away from me. Let's us have another lesson."

"Oh. Well, let me think." I knew Susannah had to concentrate hard on where to put her feet. Her heel slid in a slick of mud, but she righted herself. "Why don't you tell me what *B-R-A-N-C-H* spells."

I made a show of thinking. "I believe that spells *branch*, Susannah. Is that right?"

"Yes." She halted.

When I looked back, our eyes met, and we had an understanding between us. I would play at needing her help, and she would play at giving it. What if it really was the other way around? We weren't about to say it out loud. I didn't like the high color in her face.

"Ask me another," I said gently.

"All right." We began walking again, our heads down against the rain. Susannah licked water from her lips. "You try *V-E-R-M-O-N-T*."

We walked another bit before I could make myself answer. Twigs snapped like wing bones under our steps. "I believe that spells *home*, Susannah."

She nodded hard and wiped her eyes with one wet sleeve. "That's right."

"We'll get there. By and by," I whispered.

That wasn't a lie, not rightly. You know I had to say that, no matter what I thought about Vermont. I was afraid Susannah wouldn't be able to walk if she thought I wasn't walking with her all the way. But, oh, saying it made my heart drag wearily inside me.

The rain ran down my arms, down the backs of my legs. It was a truly miserable feeling, and I was heartily sick of it. I was cold and hungry, but I knew I didn't feel as bad as Susannah did. I heard her stumbling along behind me, and once she landed on her hands and knees. When I looked back, I saw her face was dead white with the shock traveling up her bad arm. A faint sound came through her lips. Her eyes were fixed. Then she stubbornly picked herself up and tramped on.

Jesus, I thought. Don't make it hurt so much for her.

I watched her as she pushed by me and walked on through the woods. I hefted our two small bundles and followed. It was my aim to keep her ahead of me, from now on. Branches reached out at me and plucked at my wet clothes, snagged in my hair, whipped my cheeks. My hands were numb.

"I wish I knew some of those Indian ways," Susannah muttered. "They know how to find food in the woods. I have heard they can eat bark, but I doubt I could. I have heard they have different stomachs than us, but I don't know. Maybe their physical structure ain't the same as ours—they sure don't look the same as us. You don't look the same as us neither, but now I wonder who us is."

I felt a colder chill go up my back. That sounded like fever talk. I stepped up faster and took her by the arm. She faced me, looking surprised.

"Why, Bethlehem. Whatever is it?" she asked. Her eyes were bright, like glass. "Say, I'm wet."

"I know it," I said, leading her to a big oak with a wide roof of branches. "Let's just sit down. I'm tired."

"Oh, well, if you are." Her knees folded. Then she looked up at me with sense and sadness in her eyes. "I'm sorry. I don't know what's wrong with me. I was dizzy for a moment, but I'll be fine directly."

I nodded, but couldn't meet her eyes. "How's the hand?"

"Hurts. All the way—up my arm." She pushed her wet hair back off her brow, slowly shaking her head. "Bethlehem," she said in a quiet, shivery voice. "I think I'm in trouble."

I gazed upon her where she sat, wet, splashed with

mud, and spotted with blood. Her shirt was stuck to her skin, and her shoulders were shaking. The bandage on her hand was a mess of wet and dirty strings. I felt my stomach roll over. She was surely in a bad box. We both were.

My eyes grew cold as I beheld her. I was only in trouble because of her. A burden. She had become a terrible burden. How could I hope to see freedom with this trial before me? I so much wanted to be shut of her.

But if I left her, then what kind of freedom would I have?

While she huddled on the ground, I walked off a pace or two. All around me, the trees pressed in, black and wet, their trunks streaming. Mists moved slow and sly through the woods, over rotten logs, into the hollows. Dull, dead leaves clung to my feet and ankles. With vain hope, I looked for rabbit trails and prayed there would be a snare across one. But there was nothing. All was a desolation and a wilderness. I walked back to Susannah, sick at heart. She had dozed off.

"Do you think you can walk some more, honey?" I asked, bending over her.

She looked up at me. She was shivering. "Yes."

I put an arm around her to help her up. "Then let's go."

SUSANNAH: I was a bad case and I knew it. Sometimes, walking along, I would start to feel myself float up off the ground, and then I would have to stop and grab hold of a branch, or Bethlehem's arm, with my good hand. This was a singular effect, and most unpleasant. Each time it happened, it frightened me more, and I cursed the rain, I cursed the knife, and I cursed myself for being so stupid. If I had blood poisoning, it might kill me. I knew that.

Sometimes I imagined myself a blind girl, staggering in the darkness. I would run up against branches or trees if Bethlehem didn't catch me first. This confused me. Perhaps I was blind. At these times, I would discover that I was walking with my eyes closed. I would force them open, fix my gaze upon the next tree, the next slope to climb.

Once I thought my mother was walking next to me.

"Susannah," she said. "You can rest here."

"Just for a minute," I replied, easing myself down to the ground.

Then Bethlehem's face was in front of mine. "Just a bit more on. Don't stop yet."

"No." I closed my eyes.

The high faraway fevery whining in my ears was familiar to me. I was warm in my own bed again, floating on waves of pneumonia. Only one thing hurt, and that was knowing my parents were dead. Tears came easily. I couldn't stop them.

But it was nice to know I was already home, no matter how sick. And Bethlehem was with me. "We are home," I said.

When I opened my eyes, the rain had stopped and the sky was lowering. I gazed blankly through the black and gleaming tree trunks. They huddled together in the mist, silent and indistinct, as if watching me. The mournful sound of water dripping from branches and pattering upon dead leaves filled me with melancholy. I had faint hope of seeing Vermont again.

"Here. Eat this." Bethlehem crouched at my side, offering something in her hand.

I tried to focus my eyes on the thing. "What?"

"It's fish," she said. "I cleaned it out but I couldn't cook it. The lucifers didn't start."

I let my head fall back against the tree trunk. I was exhausted. "You're forever trying to make me eat raw stuff," I complained. "You eat it."

"I already ate one. Go on."

When I didn't respond, Bethlehem put a small morsel between my lips. It was cold and tasteless. I chewed it mechanically and tried to ignore the throbbing ache in my right arm. Bethlehem fed me the fish piece by piece until I was too tired to chew. I was as obedient as a baby. I didn't have the strength to turn my head away.

"I was hoping to catch a pound cake," Bethlehem

said, wiping her fingers on the rough bark. "Didn't
see any."

"Shoot," I whispered. The sound in my ears was
difficult to hear around.

"You try sleeping again. I want a look at your hand
before it's full dark."

I let out one pitiful moan and tried to hide my hand
from her. But she took it and pulled it gently toward
her. I closed my eyes and wrapped the pain around me
like a blanket.

"It's bad, Susannah."

I gulped. "I know it."

"Try to sleep."

BETHLEHEM: Long before morning, I knew
Susannah was getting worse. She trembled and
moaned in her sleep, and her skin was hot to touch.
Every time she cried out, the cry cut through me like a
burn and left my fingertips prickling. Then she would
be quiet, and I would forget to breathe, waiting for her
next sound.

"Bethlehem?" she said when the birds began to stir.

"I'm here." I bent my head nearer her mouth. Her
breath was like the beat of a moth wing on my ear.

"Go on escaping. I'll catch you up."

Something big was pressing in on my chest. I saw
my fingers on her brow, so brown against such a

white face. I had heard of conjurers healing the sick through touch, but I didn't own any such power. My fingers were mute.

"I'm going to find a doctor for you," I said, although she was asleep again.

I backed away on my hands and knees until I was a body's length away. I saw her shoulder twitch. All unasked for came a picture to my mind—the sparrows who tangled in the nets on the fruit trees. They hung with broken feathers, their hearts racing like the tick of an overwound watch and waiting for the next unknown bad thing to happen. All for wanting what any bird would want.

Buckra. Buckra. Why should I help that buckra girl?

Susannah moaned again. Then I got up and ran.

A trail of noise and disruption opened up as I went. Quails burst from the ground; wood cracked; squirrels rattled. Each way I turned put brambles in my path; each step I took rocked a stone under my feet. The trees clawed over my head, clashing arms against me. I could not breathe.

This big thing was on me. I wrestled it silently, blindly in the breaking day. It would not release me. I could not release it.

What is thy name?
Bethlehem. Bless me.
I tripped and fell.
Jesus. Help me.

I kneeled in the dirt and the leaves until God was with me and that terrible angel was gone. My breathing quieted. A spider hurried across my hand, and I looked up.

Ahead, green daylight showed between the trees. I raised myself up and walked.

In the pasture, a white man was cutting sweet hay with a scythe. A multitude of beetles and grasshoppers sprang up from the farmer's feet, and the rejoicing swallows dippered them out of the sunlight. The man's arms came back and swung forward, and the hay lay itself down before him.

So would I be cut down, I thought. I saw this was the end of freedom for me. Never would I see the Promised Land. I looked up at the clear sky above me and tried to learn it by heart. I would keep that with me as my milk and my honey when I was caught and in slavery again.

I waded through the grass toward the reel of swallows, my legs wet to the knees and laced with webs. "Massa?"

He turned, and his eyes took me in. "There is no master but God in heaven" was his quiet reply.

"I— My—" Words would not come. I stared at him, trying to bring my throat in check. I turned and pointed to the woods where Susannah lay. "Please."

Setting his scythe down, he strode through the grass to where I stood. His eyes were as blue as

Susannah's, like the sky above me. "I will not harm thee. What has frightened thee?"

"I fear she'll die," I whispered.

The man put one warm hand on my shoulder and slowly shook his head. "She won't. Show me."

1·8·9·6

When Bethlehem stopped speaking, a vibrant silence filled the room. I glanced up from my pages. Gran was staring at her friend with such an expression as I had never seen before in any parlor in Gramercy Park. Bethlehem reached out, and they clasped hands together. My own throat suddenly swelled with tears.

Who would do this thing for me? And for whom would I sacrifice so much?

"Bethlehem." Gran whispered the name.

"I saw the face of God," Bethlehem said softly. "And I survived."

No one could speak. I could not look at Free. Knowing it to be a cowardly act, I stood up.

"I will make us some tea," I said.

My offer fell into the silence like a broken tool that was of no use to anybody. It was unworthy of notice. Bethlehem gazed at me steadily, and I sank back into my chair. The greatness of her risk put me to shame.

Her eyes had nothing in them of reproach or pride, but she stared me out of countenance all the same.

"Why did you do it?" I asked, looking swiftly at my grandmother and back to Bethlehem.

"They could have put you in slavery again," Free added.

Gran shook her head. "No. Don't you see? She never would have been a slave again after that. This *is* the thing that makes us free."

I hung my head, tasting again the bitterness of my own failure before Free. How could I ever have thought myself good and kind? How could I presume to say I loved God and followed Him? It was bitter, but I still hoped to prove myself.

When I looked on Bethlehem and Gran again, they seemed to shimmer, weightless in the air above their chairs, with their old hands, one white and one black, still clasped tightly together.

AUTUMN
1·8·5·5

SUSANNAH: When I awoke, I found a baby in the bed between me and the wall. He lay on his back looking at me, altogether quiet and placid. His eyes were blue. There was a little drool on his cheek.

"Well, I never met you before," I told him.

He blinked and pursed his tiny mouth. I heard a giggle behind me.

"His name is Nahum. I'm glad thou woke up."

There was such a peaceful lethargy upon me that I found it a trial even to turn my head. But when I did, I saw a little girl sitting beside the bed. Her hair was pulled back under a plain cap.

"How do you do?" I asked. I was confused.

"My name is Anna Tuke. This is our home. Do thou know how many days thou slept?"

Still confused, I shook my head and looked around me. My gaze fell upon bare white walls, two ladder-back chairs, one of which was occupied by my diminutive nurse, and the bed upon which I lay. I glanced at baby Nahum again and shrugged. He yawned.

"Five days," Anna informed me. "Thou must be hungry."

My stomach chose that moment to complain. I was mortified until I looked at Anna's merry smile. We both laughed.

"I am," I said. I then noticed my right hand was swathed in a clean bandage. Bits of memory flickered across my mind. I wanted to ask what had happened, but Anna seemed too slight and young to be a reliable source of enlightenment.

Then the door opened. I looked over as Bethlehem came in. When our eyes met, she stopped and grew very still. I saw her throat work.

"You woke up," she said at last.

"It was this baby," I lied, looking away. "He tosses and turns something scandalous."

Bethlehem's entrance threw me even deeper into my confusion. There was only one way for me to have come to the Tukes' home, and that was with Bethlehem's help.

Anna Tuke, though only nine years in age, owned an innate sense of delicacy far greater than her years would suggest. She hopped off the chair and slipped past Bethlehem.

"I see you're still wearing britches," I said, for lack of something better.

She didn't bother to answer that remark. She

walked over and reached for Nahum and paced with him cradled against her shoulder.

"These people say they're something called Friends. It's some kind of God thing, I guess," she explained.

"Bethlehem." I stared at her. My chin quivered. "Did you bring me here?"

"Massa— Brother Tuke, he brought you here." Bethlehem jigged the baby.

"But—"

Once again, the door opened, and Anna poured back in at the head of a seeming flood of people. At the back stood a giant of a man with a smile I recognized from Anna's face. Anna's mother leaned over me and put one cool hand on my brow.

"Welcome," she said gravely.

"My sister's name is Given," Anna told me, her hand on the arm of a five-year-old elfin girl. Given had one finger in her mouth, and she crept closer to Bethlehem's hip as she looked at me. Nahum began to gurgle.

"Thou have a stalwart friend in Bethlehem," Mrs. Tuke said. "We understand thy case and will help thee."

I was overwhelmed. The Tuke family, though small, seemed to fill the room. Amariah and Dorothea Tuke possessed a ceaseless fount of loving-kindness and mercy, and in this they so much resembled my dead parents that I began to cry. Such relief and grieving were mingled with my tears that I hardly knew what I felt. Anna, my self-appointed guardian, sat on the edge of the bed and took my left hand in hers.

Through my tears, I met Bethlehem's eyes.

My convalescence was swift and delightful at the hands of those good Quakers. Anna and Given took the keenest pleasure in helping their mother and Bethlehem feed me broth and bread-and-milk and other wholesome foods. Dorothea Tuke had skillfully checked the inflammation in my hand, and the wound was healing well. The relapse of pneumonia was soon shooed away. When I was pronounced well enough, and when Bethlehem's stubborn requests became undeniable, she was allowed to sleep with me.

"Do they treat you kindly?" I asked one night as a cricket set up shop by the window.

"They treat me the best I ever knew," Bethlehem answered.

"Are they making you do work?"

"I'm sleeping in this bed, ain't I? I'm eating at their table. Go to sleep, now."

I was learning to listen to her. Her concern and protection of me were fierce, and she wasn't above snapping at me if I overtaxed myself. I matched my breathing to hers, and with that security fell asleep.

BETHLEHEM: From the start, living with the Tukes set me so many times off my balance that I was in a constant state of spin. I was to call them Brother and Sister, and many times they bade me look up into their faces without fear of rebuke or chastisement. The little girls tagged behind me, most particularly Given. It brought to mind other white folks tagging after me and made my back itch many a time. When I had that feeling, I couldn't keep out the notion that Byron was nearby.

"Why do you follow me?" I asked Given one day while we picked squash from the garden.

She regarded me solemnly. She was no bigger than a minute. "I love thee."

"You don't," I said, considerably shaken.

Given plucked another squash from the vine. I reached to take one and tugged on it without seeing what I did, until the child ducked her little capped head near mine.

"That one is not ripe," she said with a smile.

Speechless, I nodded and let it go. Why did she love me? What could I have done or said to make this child feel that way toward me? I mistrusted her love because I saw no call for it. But I knew these people could not lie.

"Do thou love me?" was her next question.

"Sure," I said quickly, standing up and turning

away. I wiped my eye and tried to harden my heart. But she put her hand in mine, and I could not do it.

I looked down on her. We were standing in the squashes, and their bristly stems made a giant criss-cross of a spider's web. I was caught, and this little thing was wrapping me around and around with something strong. She looked up and smiled at me. She just loved me.

But it scared me powerfully to put my freedom in such tiny hands. Only other Friends came to the Tukes. They would not give me away. But ask this small child a question, and she would tell it straight. *Yes, there is a runaway nigger on our farm.*

"Given," I said, taking away my hand so she wouldn't feel it shake. "If you love me, promise never to tell a soul you know me."

Her blue eyes never blinked. "I don't know what thou mean."

Footsteps sounded behind me. I turned.

"We may never swear an oath," Sister Tuke said, gathering little Given into her arms. "The way to know God is to tell the truth in all things. To say 'I swear' may mean I do not always say the truth."

I looked down. Trust buckra to find a reason for saying no, for turning my will aside. They would not promise to be silent. I should have expected such from all my experience of white folk.

"Bethlehem."

She bade me look at her, and she shook her head.

"Never, never will we let thee return to slavery. That is the truth."

When I still could not speak, she took my hand in hers. Given toyed with the strings of her mother's cap.

"Thou have good cause to fear the white race. But thou must have no fear of any Friend."

I released my hand from hers and picked up the basket of squash. What could I say to her? My heart fought within me. Her words sounded like the Promised Land.

But it was hard, hard not to feel fear. Throwing myself on their righteousness meant letting go of a strong and well-worn rope. I knew that letting go meant falling a long way through some empty space. How could I *know* those white arms that reached out to catch me would be there before I plunged to my death? One side of me said, "Fool! Fool!" The other side said, "Let go."

"Come. Trust us as well as thou can," Sister Tuke asked as we turned to enter the house. "I pray thou may never have cause to regret it."

I prayed it, too, and let go the rope.

SUSANNAH: At last, I took my first few tottering steps out of the sickroom, down the stairs, and out into the afternoon sun. Before me stretched a sea of green corn, golden wheat, sweet hay. The fields of Pennsylvania swept away from the Tukes' doorstep, unrolling across the land their great bounty. An orchard stood nearby in its neat ranks, branches laden down with handfuls of apples and filling the air with a grand, cidery scent. I felt splendidly.

"When is it?" I asked, seeing autumn in the light that slanted in below a mass of high clouds.

Amariah Tuke stood with his hat in his hands and surveyed his land. "Ninth month, twentieth day."

I calculated and got September. The Quakers' ways were often inscrutable to me. Their *thee*s and *thou*s gave them a romantical air, like the characters in *Ivanhoe*. Yet at the same time, their emphatic plainness forbade any such characterization.

I loved the Tukes, nevertheless.

In a friendly silence, we watched Anna and Given chase Bethlehem into the barn. Their high, childish laughter flew out with the mob of startled sparrows.

"Thou might stay on here," Brother Amariah said, breaking the late, golden stillness. A crow flapped languidly across the horizon.

My heart leaped. "May we? I know Bethlehem would love it. I think she has a genuiune fondness for Nahum. He's the best baby I ever—"

"Not Bethlehem."

The warmth went out of the light as the sun slipped down. "But why?" I asked. I tried to pretend I did not know. Canada whispered in my ears with the wind, but I shut it out. Hadn't Bethlehem promised not to leave me? Perhaps, like my pa once, Amariah could make everything right.

"She is not safe here." He gazed off across the land. Surely it was hard, knowing that the goodness he saw all around him was no guarantee of a fugitive slave's freedom. He sadly shook his head.

"Bethlehem must continue North. We here in Pennsylvania have no love of slavery—yet she must continue. The Friends can take her."

A sharp grief fought in me with the evening's gentle beauty, giving to the peaceful twilight an edge that made my pleasure in it that much greater, that much deeper, that much more full of pain. Bethlehem emerged from the barn, holding a basket of eggs in one hand and Given's pigtail in the other. The little girls seemed to dance around her like fairies in the soft light. My heart clenched within my breast. This was such a good place. A home.

"Looks like I'll have to go, too," I said.

He gazed at me tenderly but only nodded.

"Looks like thou will have to go, too."

I stayed alone at the doorway while Amariah went to check his cows. A breath of air lifted my short hair off my brow, and I heard a faraway roll of thunder.

Where was I to go? To Canada, when the home I had left in Vermont was so near? I could not believe that Canada was the only place for Bethlehem. I could not believe she would be at any risk with me at home. I could not believe God so unjust. Such terror filled

me at the prospect that I could scarcely breathe. Bethlehem meant too much to me. Let her abide with me,
I prayed. I am almost home again.

The thunder rolled again.

"If you've got more sense than a chicken, you'll
come in when it starts to rain," Bethlehem said from
behind me.

"I will." My heart was heavy. I drew a shaky breath
and turned to look at her. "Why were you gathering
eggs this time of day?"

Her eyebrows set at a tilt. "Somebody told me you
need plenty of eggs to make a pound cake with."

"That's right. Eggs, butter, sugar, flour. About a
pound of each," I said. Another drumroll of thunder
tumbled across the hills. Lightning made an indistinct
galvanic flash.

"Bethlehem, we have to leave."

She didn't say anything at first. Her gaze rested
upon the land that lay draped like a sheltering blanket
on every side. The last crimsoned remnants of light
touched her face and were reflected in her eyes.

Then Bethlehem began to sing very low, and I
thought she took the song straight from my own
heart.

> "My Lord, he calls me,
> He calls me by the thunder,
> The trumpet sounds within my soul,
> I ain't got long to stay here.

> Steal away, steal away,
> Steal away to Jesus.
> Steal away, steal away home.
> I ain't got long to stay here."

"That's the truth," I said. "But I wish to God it weren't so."

———————

BETHLEHEM: We lay in bed that night, listening to the rain come down. Underneath that sound was the sound of voices. There were men below in the kitchen, and we knew they were planning for us. I stared up in the dark.

It seemed like before leaving Reids' farm, I had a kind of looseness and ease that weren't mine any longer. True, I had carried the heavy load of my slavery on my back. But that paid my debts for me. I had had an untroubled mind when I bent my thoughts toward my fellow creatures. What I did was what I had to do and no more. I had always been settled on that account.

Now there were ropes and cables tied to me from every way. I couldn't take a step without some line tugging on me or tangling my feet. Those little children. Their parents. Susannah. And now some new people were plotting to get me safe away. It might be I'd never see their faces. How could I pay off that?

This is freedom, I thought. It could break your heart as sure as slavery.

"You've got the twitches," Susannah grumbled. "I wish you'd quit."

"I'm quitting," I said.

She rolled over and put her head near mine. I felt her breath on my face. "I wish we could stay here."

"You're full of wishes."

"Well, maybe I am. These are nice folks. But rest easy, Beth. When we get to Vermont, we can find the nice folks I knew there. Emmons is what their name is. They have the farm next to ours."

She was talking to persuade herself it could be true. I knew she was stubborn enough to talk until she believed it. I could not speak against her: why should we both have broken hearts?

I made some sound that would sound like a "Yes" or a "Good" or an "I'm glad to hear it." But her words to me were like a faraway voice talking to someone else. I loved her, but I knew she was going to give me up even though she didn't know it yet. I could not tell her, either. The rain sound filled my ears; the scrape of crickets beat with my heartbeat. I was looking at the blackness in the room and feeling how hard this freedom was. I saw faces.

Lizer. Monday. Squash. Betty's Tim. Saul. Nancy. One after the other, the faces of my black brethren floated down through the nighttime shades and passed across my eyes. Some faces I couldn't even put a name onto, and those were faces from the place I was before Reids' or at the place before that one. One of those faces might be my own mother's, but I didn't know.

I had walked off and left them all behind me. How could I? How could I?

For the first time in a very long time, I felt a deep hole in me that I knew was from my mama. I'd never know her, not now; there wouldn't ever be a way.

Who was that woman? What sound rose from her mouth when a white man took me away? What did she do with her hands when her child was gone? What tears of lamentation did she rain onto Jesus' feet?

I reached up to touch one of these sad and sorry faces over me and felt nothing but air. Are these spirits? Can alive people be spirits? Were they seeing me as I was seeing them? I knew I should feel a powerful dread, but I only felt alone and empty inside. There was something I should tell them that would ease them, but I didn't know what it was.

I can read, I said, sending that thought out to wherever in the wide world my mother was. I got some good white people helping me.

I'm free.

The voices downstairs reached a kind of resolved tone, and several pairs of feet walked to the door. There were quiet farewells, and the door shut.

That's it, then, Mama. Something is going to happen next.

SUSANNAH: In the morning, we learned what our route was to be—by boat up the Susquehanna as far as Northumberland. Then overland, north, to Elmira, New York. From there, another strategist of the Abolition movement would forward our journey on.

The children were subdued—even Nahum was quiet—while Amariah itemized the plan. Bethlehem and I listened compliantly. Quakers would be our guides and protectors, and we knew we could not ask for better or safer conduct.

"It is well that you two go as boys," Dorothea said. "Society on the river will be rough."

"The captain is a Friend." Amariah looked surprised at her anxiety.

"The captain may be a Friend," she replied. "The rivermen may not be."

Bethlehem and I shifted uncomfortably under this conversation. We were both of us loath to acknowledge the potential hazards of being female. I touched my hair, this movement recalling Dorothea's attention.

"I shall cut thy hair before thou leave, Susannah," she said. She put her hand to my cheek and looked grave. "May God keep thee in His care."

Turning to Bethlehem, she added, "And thou will

ever be in our hearts and thoughts, and may God recompense thee for thy trials."

My heart brimmed. I shuffled my feet and tried to say something suitable in answer. "I thank you" was all I could manage.

I believe it was sufficient, however.

Later, we were outfitted with new warm clothing and stout shoes, a leather satchel of food and supplies, and most warming of all, a small Bible, both Testaments. To what expense the Tukes and their good neighbors were put is beyond my ken. Yet they insisted they only did right.

Bethlehem grew quieter than usual in the days before we left. I spied her out one afternoon, sitting in the lee of a fence. She was studying our new Bible. A stiffish breeze flapped the lapels of her jacket and fluttered the small white pages beneath her fingers. Her face was rapt.

"What did you find that put such a spell on you?" I asked her.

She marked her place with one finger. "These Psalms. I like them real well."

"I like them, too," I replied, settling on the grass by her. I leaned against her shoulder to see what she had read. " 'Plead my cause, O Lord, with them that strive with me: fight against them that fight against me.' "

"He will," Bethlehem said in throbbing tones. "He will fight against them that fight against me."

I looked out over the grass. The cool wind ruffled

the green blades and shivered them, bending them inexorably over. In a lull, the stalks righted themselves and seemed to shake themselves back into justification. The warmth of the autumn sun renewed itself; the red leaves blazed forth in sudden jubilation. God is great, they chorused. God is good. I had to believe it.

Then the wind returned, sending the high clouds racing along the treetops. A solitary bird fled before its might. All nature bowed before it and made way.

" 'Let their way be dark and slippery: and let the angel of the Lord persecute them,' " Bethlehem read. Her eyes looked huge to me, overlarge and frightening.

"Beth?"

She closed her eyes and took a deep breath. "I know there is a judgment coming."

I shuddered and drew my collar tighter.

"I don't know what my mama was like," Bethlehem whispered with her eyes still closed. "And for that, there surely is a judgment coming."

Her voice was the voice of a prophet. It was a matter of astonishment to me that I had linked myself to this girl. Sometimes I thought I knew her well. But at times like this, she was a stranger to me, someone bigger and closer to God's divine word. She was the harbinger of a race of giants, giants who would stride across this land in their armies, sowing retribution, reaping justice. It made me feel small and weak, as though she could have crushed me under her hand.

Some imprudent star had joined our two fates together, and I quaked inwardly.

Was I afraid of her? Or was it the chill of the wind dragging its fingers up my spine? Let no one be surprised when the storm comes, I thought. This white race of ours has called down a terrible judgment upon itself.

Then Bethlehem eyed me appraisingly. She was suddenly her own self again, and I shook off my fancies. "You finally got some color in that face of yours."

"I'm feeling pretty well," I said, referring both to my health and my present sensation of relief. "I think I've got that illness good and whipped. I'll be ready when it's time."

"So will I," Bethlehem agreed, looking out across the landscape. "So will I."

I didn't ask what she was preparing to be ready for.

Two days later we departed. In the predawn dark, we kissed the children good-bye and climbed into Amariah's wagon to huddle beneath a horse blanket. Our destination was Harrisburg, there to embark on a boat loaded with mules. These mules were being freighted up to Wilkes-Barre, for work in the coalfields and iron furnaces. We would travel inside, with the animals.

It promised to be warm, at any rate.

At that moment, though, it was quite cold. I pulled

the blanket tighter around me. The wagon wheels rumbled beneath us and bumped over the rough places in the road. Each mile took us farther away from our friends, and I felt our solitariness and vulnerability growing heavier with each revolution of the wheels. Our sojourn with the Tukes had banished all notion of responsibility from my head. Now it came rushing back.

We were on our own again.

"This blanket has a flea or two," Bethlehem muttered.

"As long as nothing worse than that bites us, it'll sit fine with me. Let's try to sleep."

But try as I might, I could not find sleep. I was all too conscious that our journey was not completed, all too aware that many miles yet stretched between us and Bennington. Yes, with all I knew, I still trusted we would get there together.

The Emmons family was more and more in my thoughts. Let me confess it: Nat Emmons was more and more in my thoughts. He had often been my companion for fishing, berry picking, and other idle pleasures. He wasn't much for talking, but I had always made up for that and more. Nat was a quiet and companionable fellow. The only faults he had that I knew about were an overliking for apple pie and a stubborn streak a mile wide. My own obstinacy was a good counterfoil. We always got along prime. I began to wonder what he would say when he saw me in my short hair and boy's attire. I practiced speeches to give to him, recounting the adventures I had had.

You'll like Bethlehem, I told him in my thoughts. She's first-rate.

I remembered Nat's green eyes and the way he whistled. I remembered how we climbed for apples and how his face appeared, grinning down at me through the leaves. Once he had tied my boot for me, kneeling at my feet, and I had looked at his head bent before me. His hair curled at the ends. He had an interesting smell of ditches and straw and cow. Nat.

"Say, Beth? Are you awake?"

"Mm-hmm."

I chewed my thumbnail some more. "Do you expect you'll ever get married?"

"No."

The promptness of her answer startled me. "How do you figure that?"

"Husband, children. It's only more to get took from a body. I won't do it."

"Oh." I subsided into my thoughts again. "But, Beth?"

"Mm-hmm?"

"Don't you think you might get in love ever?"

Bethlehem hitched her knees up and hugged them, resting her chin. "I hope not. You can do it for me."

I looked at her warily. "Well, I might. Sometime."

She turned her head. "You know somebody?"

"Nope. I just said it could happen," I protested, avoiding her direct look.

"Well, don't mind me if it does," Bethlehem said.

I wormed a finger down into my boot top to scratch an itch. Those Quaker socks were uncommon rough. "I won't," I replied.

1·8·9·6

I had pricked up my ears at the mention of my grandfather's name and seen that Gran's face was flushed with the memory of him. I had never known him. To see Nathaniel Emmons as a dirty-necked farm boy, perhaps scratched on one red cheek, perhaps cutting an apple with his knife and handing the piece to Gran on the blade with rough, inarticulate courtesy—to see this picture in my mind filled me with tenderness.

Gran had stopped speaking and was resting her cheek on her hand. Her eyes were misted. She must be seeing that boy, too, I thought.

We were silent, respecting her meanders among another part of her past. I met Free's gaze, and we both smiled.

"Well," Gran said with a catch in her voice. "This isn't getting us any further on."

Bethlehem's quiet was of a different kind from ours. Her face had in it an expression of watchful unease.

"Bethlehem?" Gran leaned forward. "What—?"

Bethlehem lurched to one side in a swift, contorted spasm and began coughing from deep inside her chest. Her hands shook as she pressed a handkerchief to her mouth, and her eyes shut tight. We stared at her, paralyzed and helpless. We could do nothing until the attack subsided.

"I beg your pardon," Bethlehem gasped. She quickly wiped her lips, and I saw her handkerchief was spotted with blood.

Instantly, I looked at Free. This fearful truth had gone unspoken among us four from the beginning: we were here because Bethlehem was sick and wanted to narrate her part of the story while she could.

While she could.

Bethlehem was consumptive. Gran knew it, and Free knew it. Now I knew it as well.

The oppressiveness of the rooming house closed in around me. Its stale and squalid odors, its air of shabby weariness fairly screamed at me. I called to mind the steep staircase I had climbed each day of that week, the dust motes floating in the murmurous dimness past one closed door after another. I was seized with forboding.

"You shouldn't be living here," I said. I found my heart throbbing as painfully within me as if I had just undergone the wracking cough myself.

"I told her," Free said, her voice low and intense. She was wringing her hands together in her lap. "I told her."

"Please, won't you lie down?" Gran took her friend's arm and helped her to stand. "*Bethlehem?*"

Bethlehem met her eyes. Who were they when they looked at each other thus? Two girls, alone together? Two girls who dragged and chased and teased each other over the hundreds of miles from Virginia? Or two women, seeing mortality take another step closer? I saw the fear and sorrow in my grandmother's face, and I wanted to weep for both of them.

As they walked to the bedroom, one leaning on the other, I felt in me an upwelling of grief as heavy and viscous as blood. Without questioning that I did so, I turned and looked beseechingly at Free. She returned my look for a moment before dropping her eyes. We were going to lose a rare thing. We both knew it.

When my grandmother emerged from the bedroom, her face was white and drawn. She plucked at her sleeve, staring dispiritedly at the floor.

"Free, if she worsens, come to me at the Victoria Hotel," she said. "She's resting now."

Free sat where she was, her shoulders rounded in on herself and her head bowed. Her empty hands were turned upward in her lap. I rose very reluctantly from my seat, my gaze lingering on Free.

"Don't you have a mother?" I asked, although I knew the answer. My breath was short. "Or a father? Any family?"

Instead of replying, Free rose and walked to the bedroom door. There she stopped and tipped her head back to look at us accusingly. "What did you come here for?" she asked. "Why did you have to come?"

"She wanted me," Gran said, her face going even whiter.

"That's not why you came," Free said. She looked on us with such pain and reproach. How could it not seem that we had brought this attack with us when we arrived? How she must hate us, I thought. Then she quickly shook her head and slipped through the door. Biting her lip, Gran led me from the room.

In the cab, Gran sat wrapped in a pall of mournful, inconsolable isolation. I longed to do something for her.

"Bethlehem must be very glad you are here," I said. She shook her head. "No."

"But why?" My perplexity was great.

"I reproach myself," Gran whispered. She raised her eyes heavenward, and a soft groan escaped her lips. "Oh, I reproach myself."

Her words frightened me. "Gran, don't. What have you to regret? She's ill. That can't be on your head."

But she would not be soothed. She turned on me fiercely, her eyes bleak. "I was so stubborn, so foolish all along. And then I could have asked her to come to me after the Emancipation. So many of the fugitives returned from Canada then, but I told myself she had made a new life. I didn't try hard enough."

"Gran, no." I could only shake my head. My throat felt constricted.

"She would have thrived with us. She would have lived with us. She would have lived." She stared out at the busy street.

The Civil War's end came ten years after Gran regained Vermont. She would have been married then and making a start on her family, which included my father. How many more calls on her heart and her energies clamored within her by that time?

Now, her bitterness and self-recrimination were such that no words of mine could solace them. That she had chosen to relinquish Bethlehem was the stone that had been pulling her down ever since we arrived in Toronto. Perhaps it had been weighing on her since they parted. Her shoulders, her entire frame, sagged with the force of it.

And a traitorous thought came to my mind: she might have gone to Canada. My face heated, wondering suddenly if Gran had done wrong, had even betrayed her friend. I hated to acknowledge it. And perhaps her strange outbursts were rooted in this maze of doubt and guilt. I had seen the pallor of her face each time Bethlehem spoke of shielding young Susannah from the truth she should have faced. Betrayal? Who had betrayed whom? What dreadful mistakes do love and regard drive us to? Why could they not speak *plainly* to each other? And yet I had failed at so simple a thing as lending an old man my help.

So many things might have been different.

Had they been, where would I be now, or Free? I

asked myself. Where will Free be when Bethlehem is gone? These were questions I could not answer, but yet they still resounded in my mind.

Gran and I maintained our silence when we returned to the hotel. She lay on the bed, face to the wall; I stood at the window, looking out at the city.

Bethlehem and Free were there, behind so many rows of brick buildings, so many streets of horses and tram cars, milk trucks and newspaper hawkers. And how many more like those two? Those many lives were lives I could scarcely comprehend. Bethlehem and Free were representative, and they were unique. There were thousands of doors in that city: open any one of them, and some great loss, misfortune, or pain might be revealed sighing behind it.

I was overwhelmed by it all. I touched the glass with one palm, then pressed my heated brow against that cool, smooth, and impartial barrier. How I wished to smash through it, if only to hear the sound of the glass shatter and scatter onto the street below.

The urgent summons we had dreaded came that night: a steady, resistless pounding upon the door. I was still befuddled with sleep when Gran threw on a wrapper and crossed the room.

"Who is it?"

"Free. Hurry."

"I'm sorry, Mrs. Emmons," came the night porter's voice. "She slipped right by me."

Gran fumbled with the lock and latch, and flung the door wide. Free ignored totally the man who gripped her by the arm. She met Gran's eyes.

"She wants you. Now."

"Please let her go," Gran told the porter. "I will take responsibility for disturbing the other guests."

I was trying to drag on my clothes as well as I could out of the porter's sight. I yanked on first one boot and then the other. My fingers stumbled over each button. My hands shook from my sudden awakening, and from what it meant.

"I have to get the doctor," Free added.

When I joined them at the door, I noticed some doors in the hall were open and the curious were ogling our private, painful drama. I cursed them to myself.

"Mary, go with Free now," Gran said. She pressed both hands to her cheeks as though trying to collect her scattered anxieties. "You should neither be out alone at night. I'll dress and hire a cab and be there as soon as I may."

Free and I hastened down the hallway, our heels making a clatter on the wooden floor. I was still trying to match the buttons on my coat as we ran down the stairs. It was only when we burst through the front door that I pulled up in a moment of confusion and hesitancy.

It was deep night. Few lights were on, and the streets were silent and deserted.

"Hurry," Free commanded, setting out down the sidewalk at a flying pace.

I looked over my shoulder. Within, the lamp above the desk glowed warmly in its small radius, its light touching wood, an inkwell, a hat. Inside was a haven from the night. Before me was a dark city. My heart quaked.

But Free had put a considerable distance between us. I thought of our mission. Bethlehem needed us. I tried to close my mind to my misgivings, ran after Free, and caught up.

"Who's with her now?" I asked, matching my stride to hers.

"Landlady. Come on." Her tone was so peremptory I almost halted.

What really did I know of her, of this girl I followed into the night? Not even her family name. What did she do outside of Bethlehem's rooms, what had become of her people, what extra burdens did she shoulder every day? How could I know her, ever? How could I know anyone?

On all sides, black and lightless brick buildings loomed over us. Distant sounds seemed to echo on a note of panic. I did not recognize where we were going, and my uneasiness and fear gained an ever firmer ground in me. I started at every noise. Weird shadows raced ahead of us from each pale streetlamp. Darkened doorways gaped at our elbows. Each figure suggested a threat, and my heart skipped at every obscure movement. I could scarcely credit that I was on the street, alone with Free, at night. The danger, the vastness of the world was everywhere.

I did halt, finally, overwhelmed by the hugeness and impossibilities I saw. It was too much. Too much. I despaired.

And then Free's footsteps ahead of me sounded in my ears. She was running alone into a great darkness, into a tunnel that held no promise of a bright end. She went full of fear, perhaps, but she went willingly.

I followed.

The rest is swiftly told. We roused the doctor from sleep, returned with him to Bethlehem, and waited out the night as he ministered to her. By morning, the crisis had abated. The doctor came from Bethlehem's room, wearily rubbing his eyes and rolling down his cuffs. He was ginger-haired, and a brushstroke of freckles stood out on the pale skin of his nose.

"She requires bed rest for now," he scowled, giving the shabby room a quick, cantankerous glance. "I wouldn't be worrying her with anything for some while."

Gran walked him to the door and spoke with him quietly. Free stood near me, her back rigid. In the growing light, I saw how red her eyes were.

"Free," I said. "She'll be fine."

In answer, Free began to shake with dry, convulsive sobs so strong and bitter and sudden that I was shocked motionless. Her back remained ramrod straight, but she dug the heels of her hands into her eyes. The sound she made was terrible to hear, there was so much anguish in it.

"Don't, my dear," I cried, embracing her. I only caused her to crumple and fall against me, weeping still more painfully. I held her shaking body against me.

"Hush, now," I said, stroking her back. "She might hear you."

Instantly, Free recovered herself and dashed the tears from her face. Her chin quivered.

"You may sit with her, if you like," Gran said gently. "Come."

We three went in to Bethlehem. She lay propped against two pillows, her eyes closed. Her face was so haggard in repose that I faltered upon seeing her. Then she opened her eyes again, giving over their vitality to her expression.

"How do you feel?" I asked. Free only knelt by the bed and clasped Bethlehem's hand to her forehead. She trembled.

"Very tired," Bethlehem whispered. She swallowed, then licked her lips. "Been a long night."

Gran brought a tumbler of water to her and helped her to drink it. "Can you sleep now?"

Bethlehem drew in a long breath. Her nostrils looked pinched. She began to shake her head slowly against the pillows. "I don't feel like sleeping, not right now. I'd rather hear some talk."

"Now, see here," Gran started.

"I'd rather hear some good talk from you people," Bethlehem insisted, giving my grandmother a steady look.

Gran shook her head. "You are so stubborn."

The way she said it, she might have been saying "You are so dear to me" or "I can't bear it." The intensity of feeling in the room was suffocating. I longed for air as much as Bethlehem did.

"Shall I open a window?" I asked, blinking hard.

"I'd take a great deal of enjoyment from some fresh air," Bethlehem agreed. "Please, Mary."

I struggled with the sash. Across the way, the faceless brick wall of another building blurred in my sight. I forced the window up and leaned out. The early morning was cool, with a touch of damp. Below me, a woman pegged wet clothing onto a line, and somewhere near, but out of view, a dog started up a high, excited barking.

"Finish the story, Susannah," Bethlehem said. "And I still intend to jump in when it looks like you've forgotten something." She pulled herself up straighter. "Free, fetch the papers, won't you?"

Her level tone forbade any further demonstrations from us. Free stood slowly and left the room, while Gran impatiently pulled a chair closer to the bed. She was clearly distressed.

"I wish I'd never started this," Gran said, working

her hands together. "Do you think I enjoy having my mistakes thrown in my face?"

"Too late for that, Sue," Bethlehem pointed out wryly.

Gran sighed. "Oh, I know." She smoothed Bethlehem's blanket and gave her friend a wan smile. "I know."

When Free walked back in, I turned. Before me, my own countenance was reflected in the looking glass and I saw our two faces side by side. She offered me the sheets of paper, and I held out my hand.

AUTUMN
1·8·5·5

SUSANNAH: The days and nights were monotonously long on board our floating stable. Our hiding
place was a cubby sealed with planks, inside which we
had scant room and little air. More often than was
probably wise, we removed the planks. The mules
would blink at us pacifically, whisking their tails and
fanning a great deal of mule-smelling air into our den.
Those were not ideal accommodations.

But we were filled with optimism, and well fed. As
an amusement for ourselves, we assigned the mules
ridiculous names such as Ironhead, Coaldust,
Annabellina, and the like.

Some days were damp, and we guessed that it
rained. Other days the air grew stifling in our hold.
These were our only gauges: we saw no sun or sky for
many days. Captain Kendall brought us food in the
mornings, as well as a bottle of water. Aside from this,
our company was exclusively our own.

That was how I liked it. We had no need to answer

for our words or deeds. We were accountable only to each other, and to our souls and to God.

How I wished it might be ever thus. As you know by now, independence in females is considered a dangerous thing. What if we should form our own opinions from the experience of our own eyes? I vowed Nat would have to look sharp, and not try bossing me. . . .

"Did you eat pepper or what?" Bethlehem broke into my agitated musings. "Your face is red and you're puffing like an old mule."

I laughed. "I'm being silly, I expect. There I was, all ready to chew Nat's head off for bossing me around, but he never even once tried to."

"That is silly," she agreed. She picked at the floor-boards with the knife. "Who is that Nat?"

I became very still and silent. There was no sound but the distant slap of water against the bulwarks and the patient slow stamp of mule hooves. Thinking of Nat sometimes made me feel disloyal toward my friend. It shouldn't, I knew, but it did all the same.

Nat was coming to seem part of the answer I was in search of. The closer I got to Vermont, the more keenly I felt what I had lost. With Vermont regained, I would have love, affection, security, all of those things that had gone through the ice with my parents. Nat was part of that past, a part I could find again. And Bethlehem could find it with me. Of that I was convinced, against all the evidence.

You see, I still thought home was a place.

"He is a fellow I know at home," I mumbled, fussing with the cuff of my jacket.

"Is he that fellow you might marry someday?" she asked.

"No!" I crawled closer to her and took her arm. "I won't marry anyone. We'll always be together—don't worry about that. I wouldn't leave you."

She smiled and shrugged one shoulder, but she didn't speak.

"Here, give me that knife," I said.

With the knife in my hands, I knelt by the planks that walled us in. I began to carve.

"What is that writing?"

"You can read it yourself when I have done with it," I snapped. I was unaccountably distressed.

She sat back and waited with easy tolerance. The wood under my knife was soft and easy to whittle, and I scored it deeply. Mine would be a permanent engraving. Through a chink I met the eye of our nearest mule neighbor, Whiskybreath. He had no more curiosity than any other mule, however, and didn't bother to find out what I was scratching on the wall for. Sweat stood out on my forehead. It was one of the warm days. At last, I had done.

" 'Friendship is a sheltering tree.'—*S*. and *B*."

Bethlehem traced her fingers over the lines as she read, brushing away the last slivers and shavings of wood. She felt it as a blind person would feel it, with two hands, learning the shape of the letters. Her thumb lingered a moment over our initials.

"I read that in a poem," I explained. "I don't remember which one, but it's a pretty saying, ain't it?"

"It is." She looked at me steadily. "But there could come a wind."

"No," I said, shaking my head.

"There could come a bolt of lightning or a heavy frost," she went on. She put her forefinger on the word *tree*.

"No!"

"There could come an ax."

I put my hands over my ears. "Don't say that— don't say that!" I begged her.

But it was too late. In my mind's eye was a vision of a barren hilltop, a dead stump rising accusingly into the air. And on either side of it, we two, facing away.

"There won't be no ax, no wind, no lightning, and no frost," I fairly shouted.

She raised her eyes to the plank ceiling above our heads. "No," she whispered. "Maybe there won't be none of that."

"There won't be," I said obstinately, picking at the carved words with my fingernail. I saw that my hands shook. "You'll just stay with me, and we'll always be together."

She understood far better than I would allow myself. That wind driving us from Virginia was still blowing, and it was soon to blow us apart.

When Captain Kendall knocked us awake the next morning, he gave quick instructions. We were to hide ourselves inside the two barrels that he pointed out to us, as Northumberland would be reached in a matter of hours and we would be rolled ashore. He left us to make our preparations.

"I sure hope they don't drop me overboard," I said when I climbed in. "This looks none too watertight."

Bethlehem looked suddenly anxious. "I can't swim."

I regretted my fancies. "They won't drop us, Beth. Besides, these'd make fine boats. We'd just bob along like two fat ducks. I think it would be quite the pleasantest part of this whole journey."

To demonstrate my confidence, I knelt down and pulled the barrelhead to. Then I pushed it aside and popped up again. "See? There's nothing to it."

She was clearly troubled by it. I had heard some people misliked small spaces. I admit, sitting in an oaken barrel with my knees tucked up wasn't quite the most comfortable thing I ever had tried, but compared to wandering through a southern Pennsylvania rainstorm in a delirious fever, it wasn't so bad.

"I guess there ain't no other arrangement," Bethlehem said with a sigh of resignation. "I come this far. It won't do to balk at a barrel, I guess."

"I guess not," I agreed. "And besides, it won't be very long. They'll roll us out on the shore, and then we'll spring right out again. It won't take more'n a few minutes. I'd say a quarter of an hour is the limit."

In fact, it took many, many hours.

Our tumbling, thunderous descent down a plank was dreadful but quick. Before I'd even begun smarting from the bumps to my head and elbows, my barrel stopped rolling. I tried to still my breathing.

Then somebody tipped the barrel on end, and I was set upon my head. I took my weight upon the back of my neck and shoulders. Never in my life was I in such an uncomfortable position, and I would gladly have traded it for my delirious fever once again.

I prayed Bethlehem was more fortunate than I.

Then we began moving once again and, by the feel of it, on a wagon.

Divine Savior, I prayed. *Make this a brief ride.*

My head ached abominably from the blood rushing to it. With each jolt of the wagon, my knees came bouncing down toward my nose so precipitously that I thought I would be lucky to escape without cracking myself a sharp one. I also began to itch in all the most inaccessible places.

But, as Bethlehem had said, it wouldn't do to balk at a barrel, not after coming so far.

However, I saw no reason to travel in a barrel *upside down*. That was too hard. I began kicking with my feet on the barrel staves and rocking forward with my body as much as I could manage. With a couple of tries, I exerted enough force to rock the barrel on edge. Each time it thumped down again, a fearsome pain blazed its way across my shoulders and up my neck.

But I was determined not to travel on my head. It was too ignominious. I rocked once more as I felt the wagon move down an incline, and felt the barrel keel over. I braced against the impact. My barrel and I rolled into the side of the wagon with a resounding smack.

The wagon stopped, and all was silent. Then we were wrestled from side to side.

"Please, mister," I whispered. The movement was arrested. "Don't set me on my head again."

Mercifully, I felt myself righted and put properly, all this transpiring without a word from my deliverer. Soon the wagon was set in motion again. The relief from pain was such that I now felt my quarters to be as luxurious and free as any red-carpeted opera house.

Every impediment and obstacle had been borne. Now I was going home, and I saw myself speeding faster and faster the nearer I got, like an iron bar sliding toward a magnet.

I pressed my cheek against the inside of my barrel. It was very dear to me. It was taking me home. Then I managed to drop off to sleep. There wasn't anything else to do.

I waked with the sound of men's voices. My entire frame was numb, and I had an urgent need to use a privy. I sensed movement outside my tiny cell.

Then the barrelhead was pried off, and I beheld a dark roof over my head. A beam of light from a shuttered lantern broke the darkness only faintly. I smelled hay.

"You may come out now," a solemn voice told me. A head was silhouetted above me.

"I may, but I can't," I replied. "Sir, I can't move."

Without comment, he grasped my arms and lifted me bodily from the barrel. My legs dangled uselessly below me, causing me to gasp with pain. I crumpled to the wagon bed, nursing my aching muscles. There were three dark figures around me.

"Where is this place?" I asked.

They did not answer. My rescuer levered the lid off a second barrel. Bethlehem was plucked out and set beside me. I took her hand in a quick grip as the men around us beckoned us to descend.

"I don't like to complain," I said. "But my legs are awful cramped."

"Rest a moment," the first man said tersely. "Then we must go."

"I can walk." Bethlehem eased herself off the end of the wagon.

I hardly believed my legs would support me, but I followed her and stood shakily on a dirt floor. A high, chittering sound reached my ears. Bats, I thought. This is a barn.

The man with the lantern turned it so that the

single beam outlined the foot of a ladder. The rungs reached up into darkness. Our hosts were still strangely silent.

"Up there?" I asked.

The lantern nodded in assent. This silence was eerie, but we obeyed. Even before we reached the hayloft, the men had backed the wagon out of the barn. The door closed, and we were alone in the dark.

I was beginning to shiver. Whether it was my muscles reacting to their release or if it was the cold or the strangeness of this encounter, I did not know. I heard Bethlehem's stealthy, hand-and-knee progress across the loft.

"There's a basket here," she whispered. I heard her sniff. "There's food in it."

"I guess that must be for us," I said.

The strange taciturnity of the wagon men had infected us. Perhaps there was some danger nearby. Perhaps they took no joy in their task but only did their bounden duty. It made me feel low and quiet.

Bethlehem and I found our supper to be bread and some cheese. There were two sour apples as well. Instead of conversation, our dinner was accompanied by the busy, nervous twittering of the bats. They came and went through some nearby opening, and I frequently felt the invisible flutter of wings passing very close over my head. I squeezed my eyes tight shut and opened them again. The darkness was the same: oppressive and comfortless.

Another bat flitted by me. "They can see in the dark," I whispered.

"So can I."

I wrinkled my brow. "How's that? What do you see?"

Bethlehem sighed. "I see a long road ahead."

"But we're nearly home," I assured her, gnawing my apple core. "It can't be too long now."

"Maybe so. Maybe so. Let's try to sleep."

I lay back on the hay and listened to the faint and uncanny squeaking of the bats. To my ears, it sounded like sarcastic laughter. Heavy of heart, I covered my head with my jacket and tried to shut it out.

The morning was fine and clear. I watched the sun come up through the open window that the bats had used. Outside I saw fertile and hilly farmland and long tracts of autumn-hued forest. A mist lay on the land like smoke, but above, the sky was as clear as the Battenkill. I started on hearing the barn door creak open.

Bethlehem was up in an instant, crouching on her knees. We shared a look silently. Slow footsteps padded across the floor below us. Then the ladder squeaked as weight was placed upon the bottom rung. I held my breath, and we waited.

A head appeared, and then the shoulders. The man turned around to find us. His pale, spectacled face showed no pleasure in seeing us. He only nodded, as if in confirmation.

"It's time to go," he said.

I swallowed hard. His demeanor was so cold and unwelcoming that I could hardly convince myself he was a friend and not some agent come to transport us back to Virginia.

"It's time to go," he repeated impatiently. His coat and neckcloth were dull black. He put me uncomfortably in mind of an undertaker.

"Sir?" My voice squeaked.

He laughed, a mirthless, silent sniff. "There is no treachery here," he said. "You move on today."

Bethlehem bowed her head. I heard her catch her breath sharply.

"Well, that's fine, then," I said, trying to instill some pleasantness into the atmosphere. I followed him down the ladder, glad to stretch my legs. Bethlehem came more slowly.

"Which way are we headed?" I asked, walking outside. The morning air held a chill. "North? East?"

The man turned his back on the rising sun. "That way."

I gaped at him and felt a foolish smile on my face. "But that ain't the way to Vermont, sir. Vermont is east. I know that."

Bethlehem walked up beside me. Her eyes were still downcast.

"Sir," I continued when he was silent. "Sir, that's the wrong way."

He turned on me. There was little comfort in his expression. "That is the right way. The way to Canada."

"Canada?" I began to shake my head and back away. "No, we ain't going to Canada. Bethlehem, I told you we don't have to go to Canada. I told you it will be fine—"

The look on her face arrested me. I found it hard to breathe as we stared at each other.

"Beth, no. Please."

"There is a community of free blacks in Windsor," the man said. "They will welcome her gladly."

I still stared at Bethlehem in dismay.

"Those are my people," she whispered. "You got yours in Vermont."

"*You* are my people," I said.

She shook her head. "You had all this time to say you'd go with me. If you didn't say it by now, you ain't going to today."

"If you plan to go to Vermont, we'll get you there," the man said to me. "I will send someone for you later. But for now, she must go to Canada. No place in these United States can shelter her."

"I can! I can!"

"Hurry."

"I need some time!" I cried at him.

"There is very little." He walked a few paces away to where a bay horse stood between the traces of a gig.

"You go home now," Bethlehem said tenderly to me, her eyes on my face.

I caught a sob in my throat. "How can you? How can you just leave?"

She looked away. Her chin trembled. "How can you not come?"

I could not speak. I thought my heart was being wrenched from my breast. It was so bitterly hard. I had blinded myself so willfully to this inevitable moment: now I was paralyzed in the glare of truth. I could not ignore it any longer.

We both stared forlornly at the ground. Then she took a step back.

"I got to leave."

I could not speak.

Bethlehem smiled at me then. "Be glad for me when I'm free," she said.

"I am."

She straightened her back. Then she turned and walked to the gig. She climbed in, and the man whipped up the horse. The springs creaked, and they were off. I watched the carriage as it rounded a rise in the track. Then it dipped below the crest and was gone.

"No," I whispered. "No!"

I started to run after them. I couldn't go home

without her. I would never regain what I had lost if I could let her go in that way.

I ran until I could not breathe, but she was lost to me.

―――――――――――

BETHLEHEM: Lord. I didn't know. I didn't look back. I had known for a long time that she would choose the way she did, but that didn't make it easier to bear, and I swore to forget her.

But I could not. You cannot forget the first friend of your life. For the first few weeks, I felt her with me everywhere I was. I heard her voice and imagined her opinions on my new people and home. I sometimes woke in the dark, thinking she was there. I know live people can haunt us, because Susannah haunted me.

Life has a way of keeping us on the jump, though. I was busy. The man who took me to Windsor was a minister, and soon I was introduced to his maiden sisters, who ran a school for escaped slaves like me. They encouraged me to put my bad days behind me and think of myself as reborn. The black family I lived with at first could not see Susannah as I saw her, and I soon stopped speaking of her.

We here in Canada followed the Civil War closely, I can tell you. Sometimes it seems to me we held our breaths for the whole four years, and what a jubilee did we have at the end! Many of my neighbors went back to their freed families, but I had nothing to go back for. My life was good where it was.

And I wanted to tell Susannah that.

1·8·9·6

Gran pressed one hand over her eyes. "I got that letter four days after Nat was mustered out of the army and came home from the surrender at Appomattox. I still have it by heart."

"Do you?" Bethlehem asked faintly. "What did I write?"

" 'Dear Susannah,' " Gran quoted, taking her hand from her eyes. " 'I'm doing fine. I'm a teacher now, and have good people around me. I hope you got home safe. I did. You can write to me at this address if you're of a mind to. Take good care. Bethlehem.' "

Bethlehem nodded. She looked deathly tired. "That sounds about right."

"Bethlehem!" Gran leaned forward, passionately urgent, and took her friend's hand. "Please forgive me."

"I forgave you a long time ago," Bethlehem told her in a low, tender voice. "You're the one that can't get over having just a plain human nature."

Gran looked angrily away. I saw her wipe her eyes. "But I could have come for you. Look at you now. I could have saved you."

"Even you couldn't save me from living, Sue," Bethlehem said.

Gran stood up and crossed the room in agitation. "Oh, how can you be always stronger than I? You were always trying to ease my load, but I've never been any use to you."

"Susannah, you've never been more wrong."

I lowered my eyes, tapped together the many pages of the story. "Free, can you—?" I began. My voice stopped, and I stood up to leave the room. She followed me.

"What?" she asked, looking back at the bedroom. She was yearning to go.

Shaking my head, I crossed to the table. "I just thought to give them a minute," I whispered.

"I know." She sat down, her chin on her hand. There was nothing either one of us could say.

My heart went out to Free as we sat there together. She would have no one when Bethlehem died. I could not let that happen. It was too hard, coming on top of everything else.

"Free, what will you do—after?" I asked.

"I don't know."

I gripped my hands together. "You've no family, have you? Where will you go?"

"I know other people. I'll get by." Free went to the window. Her expression was bleak.

"But—" I began.

Gran came to the door and paused there. I rushed to her side. "Gran, please," I whispered. "May we ask Free to come home with us?"

"Mary." She put one hand to my cheek. She slowly shook her head. "Don't you see that wouldn't work? Ask yourself, would she be happy with us?"

I glanced across the room at Free. "Yes," I said stubbornly. "She *would*."

"No—we're separate." Gran sighed. "She has to make her own way, as I did, as Bethlehem did."

I backed away from her. Gran had not stayed by Bethlehem, but I could and would stay by Free. When I joined her by the window, she did not even look up.

"Free, won't you come live with us?" I asked, taking her hand. "I know we could manage it."

She raised her head slowly and looked at me. I had never felt the gulf between us wider than at that moment.

"Please," I said.

"No." She breathed deeply. "I won't do that."

That was all. I knew there was no use in asking again. I felt empty, only a husk. There was nothing I could do. I could not rescue Free; she did not ask me to, nor even require it. She would take nothing from me.

Gran came to us and put her hand on my shoulder. "You know we have to leave today, Mary. Now, in fact. It's time to go home."

I raised my eyes to her face.

"I'll just—have a word with her," I said, looking at the bedroom door.

I went in to Bethlehem. She was gazing through the window from her bed.

"Did you say good-bye this time?" I asked, sitting next to her.

She took my hand. "Yes."

"I want you to know, when I came here I didn't—I didn't . . ."

"I know, Mary."

"But now I see," I struggled on. "And I want you to know that I think I see."

Bethlehem nodded. "I know, Mary. Good-bye. God bless you."

I leaned over and kissed her cheek, and then her hand.

"Good-bye."

At the door, I stopped and looked at her again. Her eyes were closed, but she did have a smile on her face. And I noticed what I had not seen before: the shadows and light that fell across her from the window were like the dappling shade of branches and leaves. They must have covered us all as we sat there. I smiled and closed the door behind me.

While Free stood in her place looking out the window, I tied a string around the manuscript to keep it safe for the journey home. Gran and I left Toronto that day, and I never saw Bethlehem or Free anymore.

December 25, 1960

Dear Julia,

   I couldn't read it, myself. Mary sent it to me out of the blue, and I didn't think I could take going back there again. That was a hard time. I know Mary was trying to do some good by sending it. I guess that was enough for me. Maybe I should have taken a look at what she had to say, but I just couldn't. Besides, I never have forgotten a word of Bethlehem's—she's been with me always, so I kept this whole thing in a drawer all these years. I didn't need to read the manuscript for that.

   But I wanted you to know what happened.

   All my love,

   Grandma F.

JENNIFER ARMSTRONG
has written several books, among them
Pets, Inc. for younger readers. She lives
in Saratoga Springs, New York.

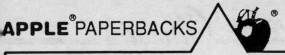

APPLE Classics

☐ MA43389-X	**The Adventures of Huckleberry Finn** Mark Twain	**$2.95**
☐ MA43352-0	**The Adventures of Tom Sawyer** Mark Twain	**$2.95**
☐ MA42035-6	**Alice in Wonderland** Lewis Carroll	**$2.95**
☐ MA44556-1	**Anne of Avonlea** L.M. Montgomery	**$3.25**
☐ MA42243-X	**Anne of Green Gables** L.M. Montgomery	**$2.95**
☐ MA43053-X	**Around the World in Eighty Days** Jules Verne	**$2.95**
☐ MA42354-1	**Black Beauty** Anna Sewell	**$3.25**
☐ MA44001-2	**The Call of the Wild** Jack London	**$2.95**
☐ MA43527-2	**A Christmas Carol** Charles Dickens	**$2.75**
☐ MA45169-3	**Dr. Jekyll & Mr. Hyde: And Other Stories** of the **Supernatural** Robert Louis Stevenson	**$3.25**
☐ MA42046-1	**Heidi** Johanna Spyri	**$3.25**
☐ MA44016-0	**The Invisible Man** H.G. Wells	**$2.95**
☐ MA40719-8	**A Little Princess** Frances Hodgson Burnett	**$3.25**
☐ MA41279-5	**Little Men** Louisa May Alcott	**$3.25**
☐ MA43797-6	**Little Women** Louisa May Alcott	**$3.25**
☐ MA44769-6	**Pollyanna** Eleanor H. Porter	**$2.95**
☐ MA41343-0	**Rebecca of Sunnybrook Farm** Kate Douglas Wiggin	**$3.25**
☐ MA45441-2	**Robin Hood of Sherwood Forest** Ann McGovern	**$2.95**
☐ MA43285-0	**Robinson Crusoe** Daniel Defoe	**$3.50**
☐ MA42323-1	**Sara Crewe** Frances Hodgson Burnett	**$2.75**
☐ MA43346-6	**The Secret Garden** Frances Hodgson Burnett	**$2.95**
☐ MA44014-4	**The Swiss Family Robinson** Johann Wyss	**$3.25**
☐ MA42591-9	**White Fang** Jack London	**$3.25**
☐ MA44774-2	**The Wind in the Willows** Kenneth Grahame	**$2.95**
☐ MA44089-6	**The Wizard of Oz** L. Frank Baum	**$2.95**

Available wherever you buy books, or use this order form.

Scholastic Inc., P.O. Box 7502, 2931 East McCarty Street, Jefferson City, MO 65102

Please send me the books I have checked above. I am enclosing $_____ (please add $2.00 to cover shipping and handling). Send check or money order — no cash or C.O.D.s please.

Name _____

Address _____

City_____ State/Zip _____

Please allow four to six weeks for delivery. Available in the U.S. only. Sorry, mail orders are not available to residents of Canada. Prices subject to change.

AC1092

SCHOLASTIC BIOGRAPHY